She'd been kissed by this man.

Sasha felt her hand being pressed. The doctor's voice. "You know who this man is?"

Confusion clouded her brain and for the first time she had a sense that something was very wrong. A tendril of fear...or panic coiled in her belly. She looked at the doctor. "Wait... I don't know...who I am... Who am I?"

Then something popped into her head. The doctor had called her... "You said Mrs. Vasilis..."

It felt wrong. Not her. "I don't think that's my name."

The doctor spoke again. Soothingly. "Sasha. Your name is Sasha and you are married to this man, Apollo Vasilis."

Irish author **Abby Green** ended a very glamorous career in film and TV—which really consisted of a lot of standing in the rain outside actors' trailers—to pursue her love of romance. After she'd bombarded Harlequin with manuscripts they kindly accepted one, and an author was born. She lives in Dublin, Ireland, and loves any excuse for distraction. Visit abby-green.com or email abbygreenauthor@gmail.com.

Books by Abby Green

Harlequin Presents

The Virgin's Debt to Pay
Awakened by the Scarred Italian

Conveniently Wed!

Claiming His Wedding Night Consequence

One Night With Consequences

An Innocent, A Seduction, A Secret

Rival Spanish Brothers

Confessions of a Pregnant Cinderella
Redeemed by His Stolen Bride

Rulers of the Desert

A Diamond for the Sheikh's Mistress
A Christmas Bride for the King

Visit the Author Profile page
at Harlequin.com for more titles.

Abby Green

THE GREEK'S
UNKNOWN BRIDE

HARLEQUIN
PRESENTS

ISBN-13: 978-1-335-14852-0

The Greek's Unknown Bride

Copyright © 2020 by Abby Green

For questions and comments about the quality of this book,
please contact us at CustomerService@Harlequin.com.

Harlequin Enterprises ULC
22 Adelaide St. West, 40th Floor
Toronto, Ontario M5H 4E3, Canada
www.Harlequin.com

Printed in U.S.A.

THE GREEK'S
UNKNOWN BRIDE

This is for Orwell, my fluffy little shadow who enriches my life and provides vital moral support when I'm banging my head off the keyboard. Even if he is on his back, paws in the air, snoring softly.

CHAPTER ONE

A<small>POLLO</small> V<small>ASILIS</small> <small>STARED</small> out of the window at the orna-
mental lake set in lush grounds. Athens lay under a hazy
smog in the distance, and the sea was a barely perceptible line on the horizon. But he noticed none of that. His
arms were folded tightly across his chest and tension
wound like a vice inside his body. A tension he'd been
feeling for months now. Three months, to be precise.

There was a faint rhythmic *beep-beep* coming from
behind him and suddenly it changed. Skipped a beat,
and became slightly faster. Heart rate increasing. *She
was waking up*. Finally.

He turned around. A woman lay on a raised bed. She
was as pale as the sheets underneath her. Rose-gold hair
spread around her head. There was a gauze dressing on
her forehead, over her right eye.

There were bandages around one arm. A scratch
down her left cheek. All in all, minor cuts and bruises.
A miracle, considering the car that she'd been driving
was at the bottom of a narrow ravine about one hundred
metres deep, a charred mass of black twisted metal.

He moved closer to the bed. Her almost blonde lashes
were so long they cast faint shadows on her cheeks. Her

brows were darker, finely etched. He frowned. Her face looked…thinner. The bones of her cheeks were standing out more prominently than he seemed to remember.

But then…looking at this woman in any kind of forensic detail was not something he'd done lately.

Not since he'd looked at her as if he'd never seen a woman before. Four months ago, when they'd first met. When her naked body had filled his vision and made his blood roar so loudly it had deafened him.

He could still see her body now as if the image had been burned onto his brain. The small but perfectly formed breasts. Flat belly, gently curved hips. The cluster of tight reddish curls at the apex of her legs. Slender limbs. She'd looked so delicate and yet when he'd joined his body to hers, he'd felt the innate steely strength of her and it had been the most erotic experience of his life.

To Apollo's surprise and consternation, a heat he hadn't felt in months flooded his veins. He rejected it utterly. This woman had deceived him in the worst way possible.

He despised her.

At that same moment that her eyelids fluttered, the door opened and the doctor and a couple of nurses entered. The female doctor looked at Apollo. 'I need to remind you not to expect too much at first. The extent of the injury to her head can only really be ascertained once she regains consciousness.'

Apollo nodded curtly, and watched as they tended to the machines around the bed. The doctor sat down beside the woman and took her hand. 'My dear, can you hear me? Can you open your eyes for me?'

Apollo could see movement behind the delicate eyelids. For a second he found himself holding his breath as her eyelids fluttered again. As if, for a moment, he'd forgotten, and a small part of him actually *cared* if his wife woke up or not.

She could hear the voice coming from far away. It was like a buzzing bee, distracting her, tugging her away from the lovely cloak of darkness surrounding her in blissful silence and peace.

A pressure, on her hand. The voice. Louder now. She couldn't make out words, just intonation. *Mmm. Mmm!*

She tried to swat away the pressure but it only got stronger. A brightness was pricking at her eyes, pushing away the darkness. Her head felt so thick…fuzzy. Heavy.

And then, as if a curtain had been pulled back, very clearly she heard a sharp voice. 'Mrs Vasilis, it's time to wake up.'

For a second she lamented leaving the peaceful darkness behind but she knew she had no choice but to follow the voice. She understood the words but they didn't make much sense to her… *Mrs…?*

She opened her eyes and light exploded onto her retinas, making her shut them tightly again. She became aware that she was lying in a bed. She could sense the flurry of activity around her. And also, disturbingly, the fact that in that split second she'd noticed a tall dark shape looming at the end of the bed.

A shape that was familiar and made her heart pound for no reason she could understand.

'Mrs Vasilis, can you try opening your eyes again? We've lowered the blinds to make it easier.'

Experimentally, she cracked her eyes open again and this time it didn't hurt so much. The face of a woman she didn't know came into focus. There were a couple of other women, also strangers. They all had dark hair and dark eyes. There was a humming noise and rhythmic beeping of machines. White everywhere. Antiseptic smell.

A word popped into her mind: *hospital.*

There was movement in her peripheral vision and she looked towards the end of the bed. The tall dark shape was a man. She knew him. 'A-A...' Her voice cracked like rust. She tried again. 'Apollo?'

'That's good.'

She barely noticed the relief evident in the doctor's voice as she took in the man at the end of the bed. He wore a dark long-sleeved top. Round neck. Soft material. Broad shoulders and chest. Powerful. But not overly muscular. Lean.

Short dark hair. Strong masculine features. Deep-set eyes. *Green eyes.* She knew this, even though she couldn't see their colour properly from here. Strong jaw. Stubble. Firm mouth. *Hot, on hers.* A shiver went through her. She'd been kissed by this man.

She felt her hand being pressed. The doctor's voice. 'You know who this man is?'

It was hard for her to tear her gaze away from him, as if she was afraid he might disappear. She nodded. 'Yes...we just met, the other night. At a function.' He frowned slightly, but she barely noticed as heat crept into her cheeks, remembering seeing him for the first time. How he'd stopped her in her tracks with his breath-taking beauty and charisma, wearing a tuxedo that had been moulded to his powerful body like a second skin.

He'd looked bored. People had hovered around him but at a distance as if too intimidated to get close.

And then their eyes had met and... *Bam!* Her heart had somersaulted in her chest and she'd never been the same since...

Slowly it was sinking in that she was in a hospital. But what was she doing here? With a man she barely knew?

But you do know him. Intimately.

She felt it in her bones, like a deep knowing. But *how* did she know this if she'd only just met him? She tried to latch onto the question to find the answer but it skittered out of her grasp.

Confusion clouded her brain and for the first time she had a sense that something was very wrong. A tendril of fear...or panic...coiled in her belly. She looked at the doctor. 'What's happening? Why am I here?'

As she said the word *I*, she stopped. *I*. Nothing. Blank. A void. The fear grew. 'Wait... I don't know... who I am... Who am I?'

Then something popped into her head. The doctor had called her... 'You said Mrs Vasilis...'

The doctor looked at her with an expression that was hard to decipher. 'Because you are Mrs Vasilis. Sasha Vasilis.'

Sasha. It felt wrong. Not her. 'I don't think that's my name.'

'What is your name?'

Blank. Nothing. Frustration.

The doctor spoke again. Soothingly. 'Sasha. Your

name is Sasha and you are married to this man, Apollo Vasilis.'

She looked at the man again. He was definitely frowning now and he didn't look particularly happy to be married to her. She shook her head briefly but it caused a sharp pain over her eye. She stopped. 'But that can't be possible, we just met.'

So, if you just met, how can you know him intimately? How can you be married?

A headache was forming, right between her eyes. A dull throb. As if sensing this, the doctor said briskly, 'That's enough for now, she needs to rest. We can come back later.'

A nurse stepped forward and did something to a drip beside the bed. Soon that comforting blackness was enveloping her in its warm embrace again and she eagerly shut out the growing panic and fear, and disturbing questions. And *him*, the most disturbing thing of all, and she wasn't even sure why.

Two days later

'We think your memory loss came from the traumatic experience of the crash. There's no perceptible or obvious injury to your brain that we can see after the scans we did, but you can only remember meeting your husband for the first time and nothing else. Nothing from before or after. Sometimes the brain does this as a form of protection when an event occurs. We've no reason not to believe that in time your memory will return. It could come in small pieces, like a jigsaw coming together, or it could happen all at once.'

Or it might not happen at all?

She was too scared to voice that out loud.

'Which is why...' here the doctor looked expressively at Apollo Vasilis, who was a forbidding presence as he stood by the window with his arms folded '...you need to be monitored closely while you recuperate.'

The doctor looked back at Sasha, who still didn't feel like a *Sasha*. 'Don't worry too much about trying to make your memory come back. You need to focus on recovering from your injuries. I'm sure everything will return to full functionality.'

Sasha wondered what her brain was protecting her from.

The doctor stood up. 'You can go home now. We'll keep in touch to monitor your progress and let us know as soon as you start to remember anything.'

That felt like a very dim and distant possibility. Her brain still felt as if it was just a dense mass of grey fog. Impossible to penetrate. And where was *home*? The doctor had told her she was English, so presumably she'd been born and brought up there.

When she'd enquired about family, her husband had told her that her parents were dead and she had no siblings. Just like that. Stark and unvarnished. She'd felt an ache in her chest near her heart but when she couldn't put names or faces to her parents it was hard to feel profound grief.

The doctor left now and Sasha looked at Apollo Vasilis. Her husband. He looked as grim as he had when she'd regained consciousness. Wasn't he pleased she'd survived the accident? He wore a three-piece suit today, steel grey, with a tie. He oozed urbane sophistication but Sasha sensed the tightly wound energy in his body. As if he was ready to cast off the trappings of civility to reveal a much more elemental man underneath.

Ironically, the one memory she did have, of the night they'd met, she remembered him smiling. Laughing even. His face transformed from breath-taking to devastatingly gorgeous. She remembered his voice. Deep and accented.

Except she'd been told that that night had been four months ago. And since then they'd been married. And she'd apparently moved to Greece from England. It was all too huge to absorb and Sasha found herself avoiding thinking about it too much.

'Are you ready? The car is waiting outside.'

Was she ready? To leave here with a man who was little more than a stranger to her? In a foreign land she had no memory of coming to? But she nodded once, briefly, and stood up, her limbs still feeling a little weak.

Apollo picked up a bag. He'd brought her clothes to change into and they only compounded her sense of disorientation because she couldn't imagine choosing clothes like this. Flared cream-coloured silk trousers with slits up each side, a matching silk singlet top and a cropped blazer jacket. Spindly high-heel sandals that made her feel even more wobbly.

He opened the door and stood back. Sasha locked her limbs and walked out of the room with as much grace as she could muster.

Apollo walked down the corridor beside his wife. She was walking slowly, as if she'd never worn high heels before, with all the grace of a spindly-legged foal.

Which was bizarre because the only time he could recall ever seeing her in flat shoes had been when they'd
met that first night.

She stumbled a little and he took her elbow to steady
her. She glanced up at him, her cheeks a little pink.
'Thank you.'

Her hair was down around her shoulders in soft natural waves that he knew she usually preferred to be
straightened.

'It's nothing.' He gritted his jaw at his body's reaction to the feel of her arm under his hand, her slender
body brushing against his ever so slightly. She wasn't
wearing the scent she usually did. He'd watched her take
it out of the bag earlier and she'd tested it on her wrist,
immediately scrunching up her nose. She'd looked at
him. 'This is my perfume?'

He'd nodded. Privately he'd always had the same
reaction when he'd smelled it. To recoil. It was too
overpowering. Sickly sweet. She'd put it back without
spraying any.

But now all he could smell was *her*. Soap and something uniquely and mysteriously feminine. Her scent
reminded him uncomfortably *again* of meeting her for
the first time when he'd been blown away by her fresh-
faced beauty. Her impact on him had been like a punch
to his solar plexus, driving the breath out of his lungs.

And to this day he couldn't figure it out. He'd seen
plenty of women who were more beautiful than Sasha.
Slept with them too. But something about her, from the
moment he'd laid eyes on her, had got to him. Captivating him. As much as he hated to admit it.

She'd seduced him with her wide-eyed act of innocence, and had then trapped him with the oldest trick in the book. The burn of that transgression and the burn of his momentary weakness for her was like permanent bile in his gut.

His desire for her had dissipated as quickly as it had blown up, and he'd welcomed it, in light of her betrayal, but now it was back, as if to mock him for ever believing he'd had it under his control.

She was playing him all over again but this time he wouldn't stand for it.

Sasha winced as Apollo's fingers tightened almost painfully on her arm. She tried to pull away and he looked at her. 'I'm okay now, you can let go.'

Instantly his expression blanked and he took his hand away, saying smoothly, 'My car is here, just outside the door.'

Sasha saw a sleek silver SUV waiting for them, with a driver holding the open back door. It reinforced her sense of being in an alternate dimension where nothing made much sense.

She stepped out of the hospital and gulped in fresh air, hoping that might make her feel more grounded. The Greek sun was warm but the early summer air wasn't too humid yet.

Sasha climbed into the car. Her shoes were pinching painfully after only walking a few feet. She couldn't believe that she wore this kind of shoe on a regular basis.

Or... She slid a look at Apollo, as he got into the back of the car on the other side, *maybe Apollo liked them and she wore them to please him?*

That thought sent another shiver through her. The thought of pleasing him. Except, if the frosty vibes were anything to go by, he wasn't pleased and she had no idea why.

The car pulled away from the hospital and Apollo exchanged a few words in Greek with the driver, who then put up the privacy partition. Sasha was so aware of him it was as if an outer layer of skin had been removed.

A hand rested on one thigh. Square, masculine. Long fingers. Blunt nails. His suit looked as if it had been made specifically to hug his muscles and emphasise his powerful physique. He looked at her and she didn't have time to pretend she wasn't ogling him.

'Okay?'

She nodded. It was a civil question but the tension was palpable. Instead of asking a question she wasn't sure she wanted the answer to, she asked, 'Where are we going now?'

'The villa. It's not far from here.'

'Have I lived there long?'

'For the past three months, since we married.'

'Where did we marry?' It suddenly struck Sasha at that moment that, if not for the fact that this man had turned up to claim her after the accident, when apparently she'd been found wandering by the road in a disorientated state a day and night after being reported missing, he could be anyone.

He looked at her for such a long and assessing moment that she could feel heat creeping back into her cheeks but then he plucked a small sleek phone out of his pocket and tapped the screen and handed it to her. 'We married in Athens in a civil ceremony.'

She looked at the screen of the phone. On it was a link to an official press release announcing their marriage with an accompanying picture. Sasha enlarged it. It was her. But it didn't feel like her. She wore a knee-length floaty silk sleeveless dress, cut on the bias and slashed almost to the navel. Eye-wateringly high heels. Her hair was teased into big curls and she seemed to be wearing a lot of make-up. Gold jewellery. An enormous-looking diamond ring. She felt a rush of exposure and embarrassment when she looked at the picture. And then she looked down at her bare fingers.

'Did I have rings?'

'Yes. The doctors said you must have lost them in the accident.'

She looked at Apollo. 'I hope they weren't too valuable.'

He gave her a funny look. 'Don't worry, they were insured.'

Sasha looked back at the picture on the phone. She was clutching Apollo's arm and beaming; however, her new husband looked anything but happy in the picture. The memory she had of him smiling had to be a figment of her imagination. A conjured-up image.

She skimmed the press release.

Apollo Vasilis, Greek construction tycoon, weds his English girlfriend Sasha Miller in a private civil ceremony.

The bare minimum of information. Sasha handed the phone back, feeling even more disorientated. A million questions buzzed in her head but she could feel a headache starting and the doctor had told her not to overdo things.

She looked out the window and saw glimpses of huge houses set in verdant grounds behind tall wrought-iron gates or massive walls. Clearly this was a wealthy area.

Before long the car turned in towards a massive pair of wrought-iron gates. They opened mechanically and a man in little security hut outside waved them in after a few words with the driver.

Sasha stared out the window in awe as lush grounds opened up around them. The driveway led up to a massive courtyard and a two-storey villa-style house with steps leading up to the front door where a woman in a uniform was waiting.

Apollo got out when the car had stopped at the bottom of the steps and before Sasha could figure out where the handle was, the door was being opened and she saw his large hand extending towards her.

She had no choice but to put her hand in his and her skin prickled with a kind of foreboding, as if her body knew it would react in a certain way and she had no idea what to expect.

Yes, you do.

Her hand touched his and an electric jolt went right through her. Reflexively her fingers curled around his. Face flaming at her reaction, she let him help her from the car and as soon as she could, she snatched her hand back.

Her reaction to him on top of the fog in her brain was too much. She resolved not to touch him again if she could help it and then that little voice reminded her that they were married.

She stopped at the bottom of the steps at the thought that they must be sharing a room. *A bed.* Her heart seemed to triple its rate. Apollo was almost at the top of the steps. He turned around and she saw a look of something almost like impatience cross his face.

'Sasha?'

She thought furiously as she climbed the steps, taking care in the impractical shoes. Maybe she could suggest they sleep separately until her memory returned? Surely he wouldn't expect her to share his bed when she felt as if she hardly knew him? No matter what her body might be telling her.

At the top of the steps was the older woman in the uniform. She was a stranger to Sasha. And she didn't look welcoming. Dark hair pulled back and a matronly bosom. She seemed to be eyeing Sasha warily, as if waiting for her to do something unexpected.

Sasha stepped forward and held out a hand. 'Hello.' The woman flinched minutely and then she glanced at Apollo and seemed to get some kind of sign because she looked back at Sasha and took her hand, saying in heavily accented Greek, 'Welcome home, Kyria Vasilis.'

Sasha felt a light touch on her back that distracted her from the woman's odd reaction. 'You don't remember Rhea?'

She shook her head, 'I'm so sorry, but no.'

The women let her hand go, eyes widening. Apollo said, 'I'll show my wife around the villa. We'll eat something light in a couple of hours, Rhea. On the smaller terrace.'

The woman nodded and disappeared into the villa. Sasha looked into the massive circular reception area. She felt absolutely sure, at that moment, that she'd never seen these marble floors or set foot in this place before.

Which was wrong. She'd been living here. She obviously couldn't trust her own instincts.

She stepped over the threshold warily, and followed Apollo as he led her into the first of a dizzying array of rooms leading off the circular hall. There was a formal reception room, informal reception room. Formal dining room, informal dining room.

The rooms were all furnished with sumptuous but elegant furniture. Muted colours in varying but complementary shades in each room. It was modern but felt classic. Huge canvases adorned the walls and antiques nestled among more modern artefacts.

Each room had huge French doors that led out to a terrace that ran the length of the house, overlooking the impressive garden. Even more impressive was the view of Athens in the distance.

Sasha walked out of the formal dining room onto the terrace. They were far above the teeming ancient city, the air heavy with the scent of the flowers that climbed the wall of the terrace in colourful profusion. She tried desperately to conjure up a memory of having looked at this view from here before, but her mind stayed blank. Apollo came and stood beside her on the terrace and her skin prickled. Sasha asked, 'Is this an old house?'

'No, I built it on this site.'

Sasha looked at him. '*You* built it?'

His jaw tightened. 'Not me personally. My construction company.'

Sasha turned to face him. 'So…you own a construction company?'

He looked at her and nodded. 'Vasilis Construction.'

Sasha frowned. 'Is it a family business—do you have family?'

An expression flashed across his face so fast she couldn't decipher it but it had looked for a second like pain. 'My family are dead. A long time ago. My father was in construction but he worked for someone else so, no, it's not a family business.'

'I'm sorry to hear your family are gone.' Both their families were dead. 'What happened?'

For a long moment she thought he wouldn't answer and then he said, 'A series of unfortunate events.'

He stepped back. 'Let me show you the rest of the villa.'

Sasha pushed aside her curiosity about *a series of unfortunate events* and followed the broad shoulders of her husband as he led her back into the hall and up a majestic flight of stairs. *Villa* seemed like an ineffectual word for what was, clearly, a luxurious mansion.

She wondered what it must have been like to come here with her new husband for the first time. A small voice pointed out that she was getting to relive that experience right now. Except, she wondered, had he been any warmer the first time round?

The villa retained that modern but classic feel throughout. Little touches of period features to give it a sense of timelessness.

In the basement there was a state-of-the-art gym and media room, which could convert into a home cinema. On the same level there was a lap pool and steam and sauna room. Not to mention the extra rooms for massage and treatments that opened out onto a lower-level garden with a couple of sun loungers and a hammock hung between two trees.

Apollo waved a hand towards the gardens, 'There's also an outdoor pool and changing area.'

He showed her his study on the first floor. A very masculine room with walls lined with shelves and books. Across the hall he opened another door and said, 'This is your office.'

She couldn't contain her surprise. 'I had an office?'

He put out a hand and she went in, not sure why she suddenly felt reluctant. The room was pretty but overdone. A plush white carpet and a white desk were the simplest things in the room. There was an expensive-looking computer on the desk.

The walls were covered with flowery chintzy wallpaper and there were framed prints of the covers of glossy magazines on the wall. Lots of shelves that were mainly empty. A handful of books.

A pink velvet chair and matching footstool. It looked as if it hadn't been touched.

'What did I use this for?'

Apollo was leaning against the doorframe, arms folded across his chest, a look of almost disdain on his face. 'You said you wanted to set up a PR business.'

Sasha looked at him. 'Is that what I did? PR?'

He shrugged. 'When we met you were serving drinks at a reception. I don't think your knowledge of PR extended beyond the service end of the industry.'

There was a tone to his voice that Sasha chose to try and figure out later. She followed him up to the second level where the bedrooms were situated. He led her past

several guest rooms to the end of the corridor, opening
a door. 'This is your room.'

She went in and stopped, turning around. '*My* room?'

'Your room.'

Apollo filled the doorway easily. Sasha's mouth felt
dry. She was aware of her feet hurting from the high
sandals. And a dull ache at the front of her head.

'We weren't sharing a room?'

Slowly he shook his head. 'No.'

Sasha desperately wanted to know why and he
looked as if he expected her to ask that question but
for reasons she couldn't understand she didn't want to
know. Just yet.

Because this would also, surely, explain his cool and
aloof manner. Why the housekeeper had looked at her
so warily.

She had a very tenuous grip on reality as it was, and
she didn't know if she was prepared to hear more revelations about herself.

So she said nothing and walked into the room. It
was luxurious, as she'd come to expect in a very short
space of time. Carpet so plush her heels sank right into
it. Instinctively, she slipped off the sandals, relishing the
relief and the sensation of the soft covering underfoot.

She was aware of the massive bed dressed in cool and
pristine-looking linens to her left-hand side but ignored
it, not liking the way she was so aware of it.

She carried the sandals in her hand over to where
French doors opened out onto a balcony that was big
enough to hold a sun lounger and table and chairs. From
here she could see that the villa had another wing, one
storey high, with a smaller terrace covered over with

trellis. The outdoor pool was just beyond this area, surrounded by bougainvillea. There were loungers and a changing area.

The grounds sloped away from here, down the hill, leaving the vista open to Athens and the sea beyond.

The full extent of this sheer luxury sank in. It was overwhelming.

She turned back into the room, blinded for a moment by the sun. When her eyes adjusted again she realised that Apollo was a lot closer than she'd expected.

Immediately her pulse quickened and her skin seemed to get tight and hot all over. The bed loomed large behind him. He looked at her with a strange expression, as if fixated, for a moment. She noticed that he had undone his tie and it hung loose now. His top button was open, revealing the strong column of his throat.

He blinked, and the moment was gone. He stepped back and went to a door in the wall, opening it. 'This is your walk-in closet and the bathroom.'

Sasha followed him, feeling light-headed and a little jittery. But those disturbing sensations and the way he'd just looked at her fled her mind when the space revealed itself and she looked upon more clothes than she could have ever possibly seen in her life. And shoes. And jewellery, in a special glass cabinet.

The clothes—dresses, skirts, trousers, shirts, jeans, leisure-wear—were stacked, hanging and folded in a room the size of a small boutique. There was every colour of the rainbow.

Without even realising she'd moved, Sasha found herself reaching out and touching a glittering lamé dress in dark blue. It slid between her fingers. It looked hardly capable of staying on a body.

She dropped it and looked around, half-horrified as much as fascinated. 'These are all…mine?'

Apollo was still trying to get his body back under control. For a moment when Sasha had turned from the balcony back into the bedroom, she'd been backlit by the sun, turning her hair into a blazing strawberry-blonde halo around her head.

Her flimsy silk top had clung lovingly to her breasts, the lace of her bra just visible under the delicate material. And he'd had an almost uncontrollable urge to stride forward and take her by the arms and demand to know what she was playing at with this wide-eyed act of innocence. She'd played that card before.

But that urge had fled, to be replaced by a far more dangerous one when she'd looked at him as if he was a wolf about to gobble her up. Instead, all he'd wanted to do was crush that temptingly lush mouth under his and punish her for reawakening this desire, which had lain mercifully dormant for the past three months, in spite of her best efforts to seduce him.

But not any more. It was awake and ravenous. And she was playing him with this little game. After all, feigning amnesia would be child's play to a woman who had feigned a lot worse.

He'd had enough of the charade. His anger burned bright and hot and he told himself it was *that*, and not desire that he was feeling.

He said in a low voice that barely contained his anger, 'You know damn well these are all your clothes because you spent many vacuous hours shopping for them with my credit card. You might have fooled the doctors and nurses at the hospital but there's no one here but you and me now, so who are you trying to fool with this act, Sasha? What the hell are you up to?'

CHAPTER TWO

'WHAT THE HELL are you up to?'

Sasha looked at Apollo and it took a few seconds for his words to sink in, they were so unexpected. But then there was almost a strange sense of relief to have the tension bubble over into words so that she could find out why he'd been acting so coolly with her.

She felt his anger but it didn't scare her. It perplexed her.

'What are you talking about?'

He waved a hand, bristling all over. 'This...farce. Pretending to have lost your memory.'

Sasha felt confused. 'But I'm not. Don't you think I want to know who I am, or what's going on?'

She shook her head. 'Why would I do such a thing?' But just then a pain lanced through the building dull ache in her head. She winced and put a hand to her forehead, feeling light-headed all of a sudden.

Apollo's voice was sharp. 'What is it?'

Sasha was about to shake her head again but she stopped for fear of making it worse. 'It's just a headache, the doctor said that they might be frequent for a few days. If I do too much.'

The recent outburst hung between them, the atmosphere charged, but after a few moments Apollo stepped back and said tightly, 'You should rest for a bit. I can have Rhea bring some food up in a couple of hours.'

Sasha remembered the way the woman had flinched earlier. 'No, I'll come down. I'm sure I'll be feeling better.'

Apollo walked out of the closet space, leaving Sasha with the throbbing pain in her head and feeling utterly bewildered. *He thought she was lying?*

She heard a noise in the main bedroom and went back out to see a young girl she hadn't met placing her hospital bag on the bed. The girl looked at her but didn't smile. She backed away, staring at Sasha as if she might jump at her, and said in halting English, 'Your bag, Kyria Vasilis.'

She left and Sasha stared after her for a long moment. After Apollo's outburst just now, it was patently evident that their marriage was not a harmonious one, and that people didn't seem to like her very much.

Her head throbbed even more, and Sasha went over to the bag that had just been delivered and pulled out the box of painkillers she'd been prescribed. She saw a tray on a table with water and glasses, and took two of the tablets.

She explored further, into the bathroom, which was almost as big as the bedroom. A massive bath and walk-in shower. Two sinks. Cream tiles and gold fittings that looked classy, not tacky.

She caught sight of her reflection in the mirror and sucked in a breath. She was deathly pale. No wonder Apollo had asked if she was okay. She looked a wreck.

Shadows under her eyes. The scratch on her cheek. The yellowing of the bruise on her forehead where she'd bumped her head.

She felt disconnected from herself, which she supposed was only to be expected. But she felt as though didn't belong here, in this hushed rarefied place. Where people looked at her as if she'd done something to them. Where her husband accused her of lying.

Why would he think she'd do such a thing?

She pushed that to one side for the moment, it was too much to absorb and think about.

'Sasha…' She said the word out loud. It still didn't feel right. 'Hello, my name is Sasha Vasilis.' Nothing but a faint echo.

She didn't need to have bruises and scrapes to know that she was very far out of this man's league. But a memory flashed into her head at that moment of feeling effervescent. Of him, smiling at her indulgently.

She'd been so happy.

If anything, that memory only made her feel more disorientated. She spied the bath behind her and suddenly wanted to wash away this confusing chain of events. If such a thing was possible.

She ran the bath and stripped off, stepping into the luxuriously scented silky water a few minutes later. It soothed her bruised and injured body, but it couldn't soothe the turmoil in her belly or clear the pervasive fog in her head.

Apollo stood looking at the woman on the bed. She was in a towelling robe that dwarfed her body, her hair spread around her like a rose-gold halo. One arm was on her chest, the other flung above her head.

One slim pale leg was visible through the gap in the robe and Apollo could see the smattering of freckles across her knee. And it made his blood run hot.

Damn her.

Damn her to hell and back.

He'd met her four months ago and he hadn't had a full night's sleep since then. First of all because he'd been unable to get her out of his head and then because she had shown him who she really was. A manipulative, conniving, mercenary—

She moved on the bed and made a small sound.

Those pale eyelids flickered open and he was looking down into two bright pools of blue. So blue that the first time he'd seen her huge eyes he'd been instantly reminded of the skies of his childhood, before things had grown much darker.

She blinked and Apollo came out of his trance, suddenly feeling exposed. He took a step back. 'I knocked on the door but there was no answer.'

Sasha sat up. He caught a scent of something like crushed roses. And clean skin. He gritted his jaw before saying, 'Dinner is ready. I can have the food delivered to your room.'

She shook her head and that bright hair slipped over one shoulder. He was rewarded with a memory of wrapping it around his hand as he'd tugged her head back so that he could press kisses down along the column of her throat, and then lower to the pouting provocation of her tight pink nipples.

'No, it's fine. I'll come down. My headache is much better.'

Sasha was still somewhere between waking and sleeping. She hadn't expected to conk out like that when she'd lain down for a short nap after her bath, but now she could see the dusky sky outside. It had also taken a minute to realise she wasn't dreaming when she'd opened her eyes to see Apollo standing by the bed. It had been the fierce expression on his face that had woken her properly.

It reminded her of his angry words. *What the hell are you up to?*

He'd changed into dark trousers and a dark shirt, open at the neck. Sleeves rolled up as if he'd been working at his desk. In this position, looking up at him, it felt intimate. An echo of a previous moment teased at her memory, as if she'd sat in this very position looking up at him like this, but in a very different situation.

'I'll just change and come down,' she said quickly.

Apollo took another step back and Sasha could breathe a little easier. He said, 'Very well. I'll send Kara to show you down in a few minutes.'

Sasha had the distinct impression that he would have preferred it if she'd said she'd eat alone in her room and in a way it would have been easier for her too. But she also had a strong instinct to try and do her utmost to regain her memory and if that meant interacting with her antagonistic husband then so be it.

'Just through here, Kyria Vasilis.'

Sasha smiled at the same young woman who had brought up her bag earlier. Kara. The girl didn't smile back.

After Apollo had left, Sasha had washed her face and gone into the walk-in closet to find some clothes. She'd finally pulled out the plainest and most modest clothes she could find. A pair of slim-fitting Capri pants and a cropped sleeveless shirt. The shirt was white but the trousers were yellow. Apparently she didn't really do muted colours.

And, thankfully, she'd found some flattish shoes. Wedge espadrilles. Unworn, still in the box.

She walked through a less formal lounge on the ground floor that she hadn't seen earlier and through open French doors to another smaller terrace. The one she'd seen from her balcony earlier, covered by a trellis and surrounded by a profusion of flowers. The view here was of the gently sloping grounds down to the outdoor pool.

The scent of the flowers permeated the air when she stepped outside. The air was warm and still. Peaceful. It soothed her fraying edges and foggy mind a little. Apollo looked up from where he'd been staring broodily into the distance, long fingers around the stem of a glass of wine.

He stood up immediately and something about that small automatic gesture gave her a tiny spurt of reassurance. He pulled out a chair and she sat down, his scent easily eclipsing the sweeter scent of the flowers to infuse the air with something far more potent.

She felt the tension between them. Not surprising after his words earlier but there was also another kind of tension, deep in the core of her body. A hungry kind of tension, as if she knew what it felt like to have that tension released.

He sat down opposite her and picked up a bottle of Greek white wine. 'Would you like a glass?'

Sasha wasn't sure. Did she like wine? Might it help take the edge off the unbearable tension she was feeling? She nodded. 'Just a little, please.'

When he'd poured the wine, she lifted her glass and took a sip, finding it light and sharp. She did like it. The housekeeper Rhea appeared then with appetiser plates of dips and flatbreads. Apollo must have noticed her looking at the food because he pushed a bowl towards her. 'This is tzatziki with mint, and the other one is hummus.'

She dipped some bread in each, savouring the tart taste of the tzatziki and the creamier hummus.

Apollo seemed to have directed his brooding stare onto her and to try and deflect his attention she said, 'Your home is lovely.' It didn't feel like her home, even if she had been living here for a few months. 'You must be very successful.'

Apollo took a sip of wine. She thought she saw a quirk of his mouth but it was gone when he lowered his glass. 'You could say that.'

She had the feeling he was laughing at her. Before she could respond, Rhea appeared again to clear the starters and then Kara brought the main courses. Chicken breasts with salad and baby potatoes. Sasha blushed when her stomach rumbled loudly. She took a bite and almost groaned at the lemon-zesty flavour of the chicken. She felt as if it had been an age since she'd eaten anything so flavoursome.

When her plate was clean she looked up to find

Apollo putting down his own fork and knife and staring at her.

'What?' She wiped her mouth with her napkin, suddenly aware that she'd fallen on the food like a starving person.

'Apparently you've discovered an appetite,' was Apollo's dry response.

Rhea appeared again and gathered up the plates. Sasha said automatically, 'That was lovely, thank you.'

Rhea stopped and looked at her as if she had two heads before just nodding abruptly and leaving. Not wanting to ask but feeling as if she had no choice, Sasha said, 'What do you mean about the food, and why does she look at me like that? And Kara too…as if they're scared of me.'

'Because they probably are. You didn't exactly treat them with much respect. And before, you treated any food you were served as if it was an enemy to be feared.'

Sasha could feel the onset of that faint throbbing, signalling a headache again as she absorbed his answer. 'You really don't believe that I have amnesia?'

Apollo was expressionless. 'Let's just say that your past behaviour wouldn't give me confidence in your ability to tell the truth.'

What happened?

The words trembled on Sasha's lips but like a coward she swerved away from inviting an answer she wasn't ready to hear yet. Especially if what he'd just told her was true. Apollo was looking at her with that disdainful expression that was fast becoming far too familiar, and painful.

'I'm not lying. I promise. I wish I could make the fog

in my brain clear but I can't. Believe me, there's nothing more frightening that not knowing anything about yourself, your past, your future. All I have to trust is that you *are* my husband and that I do live here with you, when it feels like I've never been here before.'

She added, 'I don't know what I did but if your attitude and Rhea's and Kara's are anything to go by it wasn't good. But how can I apologise for something I can't even remember doing?'

Shocked at the surge of emotion catching her unawares and making her chest tight, Sasha stood up and went to the edge of the terrace, arms folded tight across her breasts. To her horror, tears pricked at her eyes and she blinked furiously to keep them at bay.

Apollo's whole body was so rigid with tension he had to force himself to breathe in and relax. He looked at Sasha's tense body. The curve of her naked waist was visible where the cropped shirt rode above the waistline of her trousers. Her skin was pale. Her hair glinted more red in the light of the setting sun, like a flame against the white of her shirt.

She seemed genuinely upset. Agitated. Apollo didn't trust her for an instant but for whatever reason—maybe she was buying time to figure out a way to convince him to stay married—she was insisting on this charade.

For the past three months she'd been playing every trick in the book to try and entice him into her bed, but not wanting her had made it easy to resist. Now, though…he couldn't be sure he would be able to resist and if she knew that…

He stood up and noticed how she tensed even more. He went over and stood beside her. She didn't look at him. Her jaw was tight. Mouth pursed. He was about to look away but did a double-take when he saw the glistening drop of moisture on the lower lashes of her eye. *She'd been crying?* To his shock and consternation, instead of feeling disgust, Apollo felt his conscience prick.

In all her machinations up to now she hadn't ever manufactured actual tears. She'd looked close to tears when she'd turned up at his London office three months ago but she hadn't cried.

Maybe she's telling the truth.

He'd be a fool to trust her after everything that had happened, but he knew who she was now, so she couldn't surprise him again. 'Look,' he said, turning to face her. 'You've been through an ordeal and you need to recuperate. We can talk about whether I believe you or not when you're stronger.'

For the week following Apollo's pronouncement Sasha existed in a kind of numb fog. She was still bruised and battered enough not to fuss when Kara or Rhea insisted on bringing food to her room, or when they appeared as she sat on the terrace to put a light rug over her legs in the early evening, in spite of the Greek heat.

Sasha noticed that as the days dawned and faded into dusk, the women grew less wary around her. Although she still caught them looking at her suspiciously and whispering in corners when they thought she wasn't looking.

Of Apollo, there was no sign. He seemed to go to work as dawn broke—she usually woke when she heard the powerful throttle of an engine as it disappeared down the drive—and she was asleep before she heard it return.

In fact, she realised now, if it wasn't for hearing the engine each morning, she couldn't even be sure that he came home at all. A man with a house like this would surely have other properties. An apartment in Athens?

A mistress?

That thought caught at her gut as she sat in the dusk on Friday evening on the smaller terrace. The end of the working week. The start of the weekend. If they weren't sharing a bedroom then obviously this marriage was not a functioning one. And yet the thought of Apollo with another woman made her feel...nauseous.

She barely knew the man beyond some very hazy memories. And yet...she felt a sense of possessiveness now that shocked her because it was so strong. And also a sense of injury, as if something had been done to her.

'Good evening.'

Sasha nearly jumped out of her skin. She looked around to see the object of her circling thoughts standing just a few feet away. A jolt of electric awareness zinged into her belly. Disconcerting, but also familiar.

He wore dark trousers and the top button of his shirt was open. His hair was slightly dishevelled, as if he'd run a hand through it. His jaw was stubbled.

'I didn't hear you come back, I never do.' She blushed when she said that, aware of how it must sound. 'I mean, I usually hear your car in the mornings, not in the evenings. I wasn't sure if you were staying somewhere else. Do you have a property in the city?' Aware she was babbling now, she clamped her mouth shut.

He walked in sat down on a seat at a right angle to

hers. His shirt pulled taut across his chest and she had to drag her eyes away. What was wrong with her? All week she'd been existing in this numbness but now she felt alive, fizzing.

'I can't account for why you don't hear the car in the evening, as I've been returning to the villa every night. But, yes, I do have an apartment in Athens. It's the penthouse at the top of my office building.'

'You have a building.' Not just an office. A whole building.

He nodded. 'And another one in London. And offices in New York, Paris and Rome. I'm finalising plans to open an office in Tokyo next year.'

Sasha couldn't help but be impressed. 'That's a lot of offices. You must have worked very hard.'

He looked utterly relaxed but she could sense the tension in his form. He said, 'For as long as I can remember.'

'Did you study for it?'

He nodded. 'Yes, but I worked on sites at the same time, so I got my diploma while I was working my way up the ranks. I didn't want to waste any time going to college full time.'

Apollo went still. He hadn't come here to *chat* with his treacherous wife who may or may not be feigning amnesia, but if she was faking it then he had to hand it to her for stamina. She hadn't let her mask slip all week.

Rhea and Kara had told him that she'd been as civil and polite as much as she'd been selfish and rude in the recent past. There seemed to be no glimmer of that earlier incarnation of his wife this evening. Just those huge blue eyes looking at him guilelessly.

He wanted to get up and walk away. So he did get up. But instead of walking away he went over to the low terrace wall and sat on that.

She'd turned in the seat to look at him. She was wearing a white shirt-dress with a gold belt. The dress was buttoned up to a modest height.

Previously, Sasha would have had a dress like this buttoned so low that her underwear would have been visible. Then it had aroused nothing more than irritation. Now, though, all he could see were those little buttons and think about how easy it would be to undo them, baring her breasts to his gaze.

He could see her pale legs. Long and slender. Together and slanted to the side, ladylike.

He would have laughed if he'd been able to muster up a sense of humour. Not too long ago she'd been involved in activities very unbecoming to a lady.

He diverted his mind away from her dress, her legs. Abruptly he found himself saying, 'My father used to be a foreman for one of Greece's biggest construction companies. He got injured on the job, and became paralysed from the waist down.'

Sasha put a hand to her mouth, visibly shocked.

A familiar sense of rage that hadn't been dulled by time settled in Apollo's belly. 'He never really recovered. All he knew was how to manage a construction site. He could have done that in an office, in a wheelchair but everyone turned him down. His own employer refused to give him any compensation. His pride was in tatters. He couldn't support his wife and two sons.'

She frowned, 'You have a brother?'

Apollo ignored that. He felt ruthless as he told her

the rest, watching her reaction carefully. 'My father killed himself when I was eleven and my brother was thirteen. My mother got cancer not long afterwards and died within a couple of years. My brother and I were sent to into foster care. My brother got involved with a drugs and gang crime. He was stabbed to death when he was sixteen.'

Apollo's eyes were glowing with intensity. Like dark green jewels. Sasha felt pinned to the spot by them. By his words. She couldn't speak. Anything she thought of saying felt too trite. Ineffectual.

Apollo continued. 'I made it my life's mission to go after the man who had employed my father and cast him aside like a piece of unwanted trash. And I succeeded. It didn't take much to dismantle his business because he was corrupt to the core. As soon as he went down, hundreds of disgruntled ex-employees came out of the woodwork looking for compensation and that's what ruined him in the end.'

He was looking at her now as if he expected her to be shocked. And she was. 'I'm sorry,' she said huskily. 'I can't imagine what it must have been like to lose so many when you were so young. I don't know about my family...when my parents died.'

Apollo was reeling that he'd let all of that tumble from his mouth. A bare handful of people knew about his past, and yet he'd just told Sasha everything. The one person in the world that he should trust the least. He waited for the mask to slip, for her to take advantage of sharing his sad story. But it didn't.

She'd gone pale. And her eyes were huge. And she

was frowning now. 'You said my parents are dead, and I've no siblings?'

He nodded. 'You told me that your mother was a single parent. Your father left when you were small. You looked for him but found out that he'd died some years ago and then your mother died a couple of years ago.'

'Oh…it's so strange not to be able to remember my mother. Or looking for my father.'

She seemed to be genuinely tortured. Biting her lip. Apollo had a sudden flashback to kissing her for the first time, feeling the cushiony softness of her mouth opening under his, allowing him to delve deeper…all the way… His hands curled tight around the lip of the wall in a bid to douse the growing inferno in his blood.

He stood up. 'I have some work calls to make. Goodnight, Sasha.'

She looked distracted. 'Goodnight.'

He was walking out but he couldn't get those huge bruised-looking eyes out of his head. He stopped at the door and looked back. She cut a curiously vulnerable figure on the large couch.

'I'm sorry about your parents.'

She turned around and some of that vivid gold and red hair slipped over her shoulder. 'Thank you.'

Desire squeezed Apollo like a vice. He wanted to go back over there and pull apart that flimsy dress material and spread it wide so he could see her pale beauty. He wanted to force her to admit that she was just acting. Messing with his head again. He wouldn't make love to her. He'd have her begging for it and then he'd leave her there, panting and admitting who she really was.

'Goodnight, Sasha.'

Apollo walked out before he followed his base instincts and did something stupid because that way lay madness. The same madness that had made him want her with a primal need he'd never felt before, the first time he'd looked at her.

He got to his study and poured himself a drink and sat down, unable to excise the image of those huge blue eyes out of his brain. Or the impact they'd had on him the first time he'd seen her.

That night, in that anonymous function room in London, had been the first time that anyone had managed to slip past Apollo's defences so skilfully, and without even trying. By just looking at him. Something wild and untamed had crackled to life inside him and he'd realised that he'd never truly felt desire before. He'd taken many lovers but had never allowed them to get close. Satisfying his physical urges only.

After his experiences—seeing his father humiliated and belittled and ultimately destroyed; after seeing his mother wither and fade from their lives, a sad broken woman; and after watching his brother self-destruct— Apollo had vowed never to let anyone close enough to make him care when they would inevitably leave. He'd been left behind too many times.

But for the first time, with Sasha, satisfying his physical urges had taken on a whole new level of need. He'd had to have her. And so he'd followed his base instincts and indulged.

He'd lost himself in her before he'd come back to his senses. And remembered who he was. And what he was. And what he was was empty inside.

Revenge had filled that space for a long time. He'd

only been coming to terms with the fact that it hadn't felt more cathartic to have achieved his goals when he'd met Sasha. He'd put her effect on him down to that curious space he'd been in. Anticlimactic. Restless. Dissatisfied, when he should have been satisfied. At peace.

There was a knock on his door and he tensed. 'Come in.'

Sasha took a deep breath outside Apollo's study door. She knew he'd said he was taking or making calls but she hadn't heard his voice when she'd diverted to his office en route to her bedroom, so she'd acted on impulse.

She opened the door and he was sitting behind his desk, a brooding expression on his face. He frowned. 'Is everything okay?'

She nodded, but immediately regretted her decision when that awareness of him coiled tight, down low in her belly. 'Fine. I just...' She stopped. She shouldn't have come here now. The way he made her feel just by looking at her was so...disturbing. She wanted to run but also stay rooted to the spot.

He frowned. 'Sasha—'

She spoke in a rush. 'I know you're busy, but I want to know why our marriage is...like this. Separate bedrooms. Tense. You don't like me very much.'

At all, whispered a little voice.

Apollo put down the glass in his hand. He stood up and came around to sit on the edge of his desk. Arms folded across his chest, which only drew attention to his muscles. Heat washed up through her body and she couldn't stop it.

Had she always been so aware of men?

Maybe it's just him, whispered a voice.

Somehow, she couldn't deny that it was entirely possible she only reacted like this to him.

Apollo saw the twin flags of colour in Sasha's cheeks. He was almost disappointed that she was showing her true colours again so soon. She'd nearly had him convinced. But coming here like this now…she must have seen his desire for her. And now she was taking advantage of it.

He was tempted to just confront her right now, but something in him counselled against acting too hastily. 'Our marriage had some…issues, but I don't think now is the time to go into them.'

He watched her carefully, which only made him more aware of her. Aware that he wanted her.

Witch.

She looked at him. 'I don't know why but I feel I need to apologise, as if I've done something wrong and that's why you hate me and Rhea and Kara look at me as if I'm about to do something unexpected.'

Apollo fought the pull to believe her. To trust in this image of innocence she was putting forward. She'd done it before. He straightened up from the desk. He told himself he was moving closer to test her, just to see if she would show her true colours. Not because he wanted to.

Her eyes got big and round and the pink in her cheeks deepened as she looked up at him as if he were a big bad wolf. Something snapped inside Apollo, some control he'd been exerting since she'd woken in the hospital bed and looked at him with those blue eyes, re-igniting his desire.

He reached out and caught a lock of her hair, winding

it around his finger. It felt like silk. It reminded him of how it had felt when her hair had trailed over his naked chest the night they'd made love.

'I prefer it like this, loose and wild. You preferred it straightened.'

'I did?' Sasha's chest constricted. Why couldn't she seem to breathe? The air was thick and full of something that felt alive. The awareness she felt turned into a pulse in her blood. Heavy and persistent.

Almost as if he was talking to himself, Apollo said, 'It was like this the night we met.'

'I don't… I don't remember. I mean, I remember bits of that night but not details…'

Apollo stood in front of her, eyes roving her face. 'Are you sure, Sasha? Really? Or is this just an elaborate stunt to gain my trust? To get back into my bed?'

His words acted like cold water in her blood. She pulled back, dislodging his hand from her hair. '*No.* I wouldn't do that.'

He moved closer again and put his hand under her chin, tipping her face up. So much for his words dousing the heat. It sizzled back at his touch, just as potent.

'Wouldn't you? It's no less than you've already done, but I have to admit, if you are acting, your skills are exemplary.'

For the first time since she'd woken up in the hospital something more than confusion and bewilderment rushed through her, distracting her. Sasha took his hand to pull it down. 'Maybe that's because I'm not acting.'

But instead of pushing his hand away to break all contact with him and his cynical words, she couldn't seem to let go. Electricity hummed through her, mixing with the high emotion to create a volatile mix.

For a crazy second she almost thought he was going to kiss her. But then he broke contact and stepped back. His eyes were so dark in the dim light they looked black. Sasha felt a little dizzy, as if they *had* kissed.

He said curtly, 'You should go to bed, Sasha. It's late.' He went to the door and held it open.

Sasha couldn't understand what had just come over her. The depth of the need to have him kiss her still left her shaken.

Dear God, had she actually asked...?

She all but ran out of his office before she could read the disgust on his face or, worse, let him see the awful surge of humiliation climbing up from her gut.

Apollo waited until Sasha had disappeared before closing his door. He went back to his desk and downed his drink in one, as if that might burn away how close he'd come to taking what she was offering, lifting that lush mouth towards him, begging with those huge eyes to kiss her.

One minute he'd been wondering how she'd managed to sneak under his guard again, and the next he'd been on the verge of hauling her closer to relive that night they'd shared—which was exactly what she'd been angling for since they'd married.

His hand tightened around the crystal glass so much he had to relax for fear of breaking it.

Sexual frustration bit sharply into his gut. He'd spent the last three months without so much as a flicker of arousal when he'd looked at his wife. And now it wasn't a flicker. It was an inferno.

He couldn't understand what was happening. But he knew that, no matter how intense it got, he would not be weak. He'd been weak for her once before and she'd upended his life. It wouldn't happen again.

CHAPTER THREE

SASHA WENT UPSTAIRS to her bedroom, feeling dazed. She stood in the middle of the room and put her fingers to her mouth, almost as if to test that they hadn't kissed, it had felt so real, so inevitable. But, no, her mouth was the same. Not swollen. Throbbing with sensation.

Because she knew what that felt like.

It hit her then, like a sledgehammer. She'd wanted it so badly because she knew what it felt like to be kissed by him. That's why her body had literally ached…from the memory of knowing his touch. Wanting it again.

She sat down on the end of her bed, going cold inside. Thank God he'd pulled back before she'd have been able to articulate her need any more than she already had, silently. She cringed to think of how he'd put his hands on her arms, literally pushing her away.

She realised something else. Maybe she'd craved it so badly because it had felt familiar to her body to be kissed by him. And since everything else around her was so unfamiliar she'd gravitated towards that. A natural response of her body to seek anything familiar?

And exciting, whispered a little voice.

It didn't give her much relief to put it into this context. A flimsy justification for what had nearly happened.

And with a man who resented her presence and had told her to her face that he didn't trust her. What kind of a masochist was she?

When Sasha made her way down to breakfast the next morning she felt ragged. She'd woken at dawn, sweaty, tangled in her sheets. Dissatisfied. She'd slept fitfully and her dreams had been full of X-rated images. Images that she couldn't be sure now *were* just from her dreams. They'd felt like memories...

When she walked onto the small terrace where she'd eaten breakfast alone all week, she wasn't prepared to see Apollo. She hadn't heard his car that morning but she'd still been hoping she might have missed it. But then she realised it was a Saturday so he must be off work.

He looked up at her as he lifted a coffee cup to his mouth, but immediately put it down again and stood up. There was no discernible expression on his face.

She avoided his eye, hating the way her body prickled all over with the same heat she'd felt last night. She almost resented his presence, which was ridiculous when it was his house.

Their house.

But it didn't feel like her house. 'Good morning.'

'Kalimera.'

Sasha sat down and Rhea appeared with coffee, which she poured into a cup for Sasha.

Sasha smiled tentatively at her and said carefully, *'Efharisto.'*

Rhea nodded her head and smiled. When she was gone Apollo said, 'You've been learning Greek?'

Sasha picked up a pastry, anything to avoid looking at Apollo and reliving that moment last night when she'd all but begged him to kiss her. 'Just a few everyday words. Kara helps me.'

'You didn't seem inclined to want to pick it up before.'

Sasha's knife stilled. She looked at Apollo. 'Can we agree that perhaps things might be different now? You keep telling me things I did, or the way I was, and I can't remember any of it. Can we just...go forward from here?'

He looked at her for a long moment. So long that she felt her face get hot. Eventually he inclined his head. 'Very well. That's fair.'

Sasha breathed out.

'How are you feeling now? Physically?'

She took a gulp of coffee, composing herself. 'I'm fine...much better. Physically.' She made a face. 'Mentally...the fogginess has gone but now it's just a great big blank.'

And the way you make me feel like I'm plugged into some hot electrical force.

She clamped her mouth shut in case the words fell out.

Apollo wiped his mouth with a napkin. 'I've arranged for the doctor to come this morning to check you over.'

Sasha's gut clenched. Was he trying to get rid of her? What would happen once she was well enough? Why did she feel sick at the prospect when he obviously resented her presence? Impulsively she asked, 'Was it ever good? Between us?'

Apollo put his hand on the table, face unreadable. 'Briefly.'

The thought of him wanting her as much as she'd wanted him last night was too overwhelming to contemplate for a moment. She struggled to understand. 'But…then why—?'

'Didn't it work?' His voice was harsh.

Sasha nodded. Just at that moment Rhea appeared and Sasha cursed the interruption.

Rhea said, 'The doctor is here to see Kyria Vasilis.'

Apollo looked at Rhea and smiled. A proper smile. The first smile Sasha had seen on his face. Her heart flip-flopped. It transformed him from merely gorgeous to devastating.

But then he looked back at her and it faded. Sasha felt a chill breeze up her spine. He really hated her. For whatever she had done. And a moment ago she'd been ready to hear it but now she was glad of the interruption.

'Physically you've made a remarkable recovery, Mrs Vasilis. Emotionally, how are you doing?'

Sasha tucked her shirt back into her trousers. The doctor had seen her in her bedroom. The same kind female doctor who had attended to her in the hospital after the accident.

She sat down on a chair by the writing desk, aware of the doctor's keen dark eyes on her. 'I'm… I guess I'm okay. Getting used to my life.'

And the husband who doesn't want me here.

The doctor nodded. 'I can imagine it'll take some adjustment. And your memory...anything coming back yet?'

Sasha shook her head. 'Not really. It's just all blank. But I had dreams last night.' She stopped, blushing.

The doctor said, 'Go on, my dear.'

Embarrassed to have mentioned this, Sasha said, 'It's just that they felt like memories more than a dream. Of me and my husband.'

The doctor nodded. 'That could very well be the case. I'd advise you to keep a notebook by the bed, write down your dreams and that could help jog something. But don't put too much pressure on yourself, our minds work in mysterious ways.'

The doctor stood up and Sasha stood too. 'There was something else.'

'Oh?' The doctor was putting things back into her bag. She stopped.

'I just... My husband tells me that I'm behaving differently from how I was before. Would that be normal?'

The doctor considered this and then said slowly, 'It has been known...for head trauma injuries to cause some kind of personality change but we saw no indication of such trauma in your brain scan. You just got a very hard knock to the head. It's just going to take time to readjust to your life, Mrs Vasilis. Don't worry, and let me know as soon as there are any developments with your memory.'

By the time Sasha had waved the doctor off, it was late morning. She turned around to see Kara adjusting a vase of exotic blooms on the table in the middle of the hall. Sasha walked over, 'Have you seen Apo— my husband?'

Kara nodded, 'He left a little while ago for the office. He said to tell you he'd be home later this afternoon.'

'Oh.' Silly to feel so disappointed. She wasn't even sure what she would have done if he had been here.

Feeling her way, she said, 'He seems to work a lot.'

Kara looked at her and rolled her eyes. 'Always he is working. Morning, noon and night, except before we thought it was because—'

Suddenly she stopped and Sasha felt a burn of humiliation rise up inside her.

To get away from her?

She swallowed it down. 'Thank you, Kara. The truth is I'm not sure what to do with myself. What did I normally do?'

Kara avoided her eye, clearly embarrassed. 'You liked shopping, a lot.' Sasha's heart sank at the thought of shopping. What could she possibly need?

'Was there anything else?'

The young girl's face brightened. 'You could go and lie by the pool, you like that.'

'I do?'

Apollo walked into the gardens towards the pool, where he'd been told Sasha had been all afternoon. Maybe she'd finally cracked and was showing her true colours again. He'd found her by the pool countless times before, surrounded by the detritus of afternoon snacks and sugary drinks. Dog-eared magazines.

Once he'd questioned whether it was good for her, but that had been before he'd found out about— He came to an abrupt standstill as he rounded the bush that artfully hid the pool from prying eyes.

Apollo lifted his sunglasses onto his head. Sasha lay on a sun bed under an umbrella. At first he thought she was naked and his blood rushed straight to his groin. It wouldn't be the first time. She'd habitually sunbathed topless, scandalising Rhea. Trying to tempt him. Not that it had worked.

But, no, he realised she wasn't naked. She wasn't far from it though, in a flesh-coloured one-piece, which was low-cut enough to reveal the plump pale flesh of her breasts. He could already imagine what it might look like if she stepped out of the pool, her red hair slicked back like a wet flame down her back. The clingy material would leave nothing to the imagination. The way her nipples would have gone hard in the water, pressing against the—

Christos.

Disgusted at his lack of control, Apollo tore his gaze off his wife's body. There was no detritus around her. Just a book. And a glass of water.

He could still recall how close he'd come to hauling her against his body last night, crushing that rosebud mouth under his. He could try to convince himself that he'd just been testing her, but he knew his motivations went much deeper and darker than that.

He wanted her again.

When his assistant in London had told him that she was waiting to see him three months ago, a month had passed since their night together. She'd been on his mind constantly, especially at night, when he'd got used to waking from erotic dreams, aching with frustration.

He'd taken more cold showers in that period than he'd ever taken in his whole life.

And he hadn't been able to stem the tide of something that had felt a lot like…relief. That she'd been the one to make the move. To expose herself for wanting more.

But then as soon as she'd walked into his office that day, he'd felt…nothing. Less than nothing. Not a blip of response. Even though she'd looked exactly the same. Fresh face. Hair loose around her shoulders. Innocent. Tremulous.

He hated to admit it now but relief his desire for her had waned hadn't been the overriding sentiment. It had been a sense of disappointment. Because it was proof that she wasn't different from any other woman he'd slept with. And that what they'd shared that night couldn't have possibly been as amazing as he'd remembered it. Amazing enough to make him regret telling her—

Suddenly her body jerked on the bed and a sound came out of her mouth, like a cry. Indistinct words. Something like, *'No, please don't stop!'*

Before Apollo knew what he was doing he'd come down beside the bed, two hands on Sasha's bare arms. They felt impossibly slender. Her body was tense all over, he could see a slight sheen of perspiration on her skin. His insides clenched with an emotion he didn't want to name.

'Sasha…wake up.'

Apollo's hands were on her skin. Burning. She ached all over with a hunger she'd felt only once before. It was

*so clear now. She needed him to assuage that hunger...
to make her come alive—*

'Sasha!'

Sasha opened her eyes and all she could see were the
deepest pools of green. A kind of green that made her
think of mysterious oceans. Vast. Impenetrable.

'You were dreaming.'

Apollo's voice. Hard. Unyielding. Suddenly Sasha's
consciousness snapped back. She was on the lounger.
She'd fallen asleep. But Apollo still had his hands on
her. She could smell his scent. See the stubble on his
jaw. She wanted to reach out and see how it felt. She
imagined it would prickle against her skin.

She remembered how that felt.

Dreams and the present moment were meshing disturbingly and she felt disorientated.

She sat up abruptly, dislodging his hands. He stood
up. She reached for the robe, pulling it on awkwardly,
very conscious of the revealing swimsuit. It had been
the only one-piece she could find in a sea of brightly
coloured string bikinis.

'Apollo, I didn't hear you. What time is it?'

Sasha looked deliciously tousled, cheeks flushed,
eyes sleepy. Apollo gritted his jaw as his eyes tracked
her movements, her small breasts high and firm under
the stretchy material. She was so pale her skin was almost translucent. He frowned. She'd been more tanned
before. But, of course, it must have been fake. A welcome reminder of who he was dealing with. Memory
loss or no memory loss.

The lingering tendrils of concern for her distress

made his voice harsh. 'You should watch yourself in the sun,' he said. 'You can burn even in the shade.'

Sasha flinched inwardly at his abrupt tone, belting the robe tightly around her. The robe chafed against her tingling skin. She could still feel the imprint of his hands on her arms. Defensively she said, 'I found sun block in the bathroom, of course I put some on. I may have lost my memory but I'm not clueless about the dangers of the sun.'

She risked looking up at Apollo now that she was covered up again, diverting her mind from the vividly disturbing dream. He was wearing a short-sleeved polo shirt and cargo shorts. Unexpectedly casual and effortlessly sexy.

He said, 'I just came to tell you that I'm going out this evening.'

'Oh.' It was strange but for the first time she was aware she hadn't left the confines of this estate since her return from the hospital. She had a sense of claustrophobia. 'Where are you going?'

'It's a charity ball, in aid of research into cancer.'

For some reason that struck a chord with Sasha and for a moment something hovered on the edge of her mind but then it was gone.

She stood up. 'Should I come with you?'

He shook his head. 'No need. I'm just letting you know I won't be here for dinner.'

It wasn't as if they'd been having cosy dinners all week but Apollo was the only constant familiar thing in her world right now and she was determined to try and improve relations. What else could she do? She couldn't continue to exist in this limbo where they circled each other like suspicious foes.

She still didn't know exactly what had happened between them and she wasn't even sure if she wanted to know what she'd done to lead to this impasse, but she could work with what she had. She wanted to at least try to mend bridges.

'Didn't I go to events with you? As your wife?'

Apollo searched for any hint of a crack in her facade but she looked utterly guileless. Did she really not remember saying to him, 'Why not use me? Surely it's better for you to be seen with a wife than not? It'll help your business to be seen as more settled.'

When they'd married, he hadn't had any intention of involving her in his life more than he'd had to, but he'd had to admit that on some level she was right. And so he'd taken her to a couple of events.

Sasha was looking at him now. 'What is it? Why are you looking at me like that?'

'You don't remember?'

She went pale. 'No. What did I do?'

'Let's just say that you ruffled some feathers.'

'How?'

'You were rude to staff and visibly bored when you realised that the social and corporate events I attend aren't generally designed for entertainment purposes.'

Sasha felt queasy. Was there anything she had done right? 'I can't keep apologising for things I can't remember. But maybe this is an opportunity to make it up to you. No matter what I did, won't your friends and colleagues be wondering where your wife is?'

He didn't refute her question so she asked, 'What

time do you have to leave? It won't take me long to get ready.'

He arched a brow. 'I'll believe that when I see it.' He put his sunglasses back over his eyes and without that laser-like gaze stripping her bare she breathed easier.

'I have to leave in an hour. If you're coming, be downstairs waiting for me, or I go alone. I won't wait, Sasha.'

Less than an hour later, Sasha waited nervously downstairs in the main hall for Apollo. After his ultimatum she'd panicked. She had no idea how on earth to get ready for such an event. She'd found Kara in the kitchen and had begged the young woman to come with her to help her. Initially she had been reluctant but then she'd relented, telling Sasha that Apollo had asked for his tuxedo to be ready for him so at least they knew it was black-tie.

They'd managed to find a dress that was suitable and not too revealing, and Kara had helped with her hair and make-up. And now Sasha stood here, wondering what on earth she'd been doing, saying she'd go along to an event—she had no idea if she would be able to handle herself in such a milieu. She'd been serving drinks when she'd met him, not drinking them!

She would make a fool of herself and any hope she had of redeeming herself in Apollo's eyes would be gone. And what deeper impulse was whispering to her to look for redemption? Then what? Did she want him to like her again?

Want her again?

Panic gripped her. She couldn't do this. She turned

to flee back to her room before Apollo saw her—he'd obviously not expected her to be ready anyway. But it was too late. He was at the top of the stairs and staring at her as if she were a total stranger. Her own eyes widened and her chest constricted as the air rushed out.

He was wearing a classic black tuxedo. White shirt, black bow-tie. She was not prepared for his impact on her. And yet she'd seen him like this before, the first night they'd met. A vivid flashback assailed her before she knew what was happening—Apollo had been helping her with her heavy tray of drinks and she'd been laughing and getting hot with embarrassment. 'Honestly, I'm fine. If my boss sees you helping me, I'll get into trouble.'

He'd kept hold of the tray, 'I'm not letting go unless you agree to come for a drink with me afterwards.'

She'd seen her boss then, across the room, clocking her. Terrified she'd lose the job, she'd said, 'Okay, fine! Now, please…let me go.'

That memory faded but, as easily as if it had been there all the time, just hiding behind a curtain, she now remembered that evening, and fragmented images from another evening, a date…going for dinner with him in a beautiful restaurant in a tall glittering building with London laid out before them, a sea of twinkling lights… She'd been so excited. Nervous. Incredulous.

Happy…

Apollo couldn't believe what he was seeing. Sasha, waiting for him. Ready. And looking presentable. More than presentable.

Beautiful.

She was wearing a black silk one-shouldered dress, with ornate silk flowers trailing over one shoulder. Cut on the bias, the dress fell in soft billowing folds to the floor.

A braid framed one side of her face and her hair was pulled back into a low bun. It was all at once pretty and youthful but also elegant. Discreet diamonds shone in her ears. Her hands and throat were bare. Her make-up was minimal.

The starkness of the black dress only served to highlight her delicate fair colouring. Those vivid blue eyes. It was a far cry from her usual style, which was showing as much skin as possible, with lots of make-up, jewellery and big hair.

Desire pulled taut like a drum inside him. He had to force himself to move down the stairs. When he got close, her eyes were huge, on him, as if she'd never seen him before. She looked pale and he could see that her fingers were holding her clutch bag so tight her knuckles were white.

'What is it? Are you okay?'

She swallowed and nodded jerkily. She sounded a bit breathless. 'I just… I just remembered London. More about that night we met. And another night?'

He nodded slowly. 'I took you out the following evening for dinner.'

'We were in a building…it looked like a piece of broken glass.'

'The Shard?'

She nodded. 'Yes. I still don't remember much else beyond that building, the view…but it's a start.'

Something uneasy moved through Apollo. If she *was*

acting then she'd gone beyond a point that most people could keep up a pretence. He said carefully, 'That's good.'

A little colour came back into her cheeks and now she looked nervous. She gestured to the dress. 'Is this okay? I wasn't sure... Kara helped me.'

'Kara?'

She nodded and then looked worried. 'Is that a problem? Shouldn't I have asked her?'

Apollo, for the first time, had to bite back a smile. 'On the contrary, she tried to help you before but you insisted on getting in a professional stylist.'

Sasha looked tortured. 'I had no idea. I should apologise.' She made to go towards the kitchen but Apollo caught her hand, aware of how small it felt in his.

'It's not that big a deal, you can tell her another time.' But he couldn't seem to let her hand go. His gaze swept up and down, taking in the way the swells of her breasts pushed against the thin fabric of the dress. He wondered if she was wearing a bra—imagined cupping one firm weight in his hand, feeling the stab of her nipple— He shut down his rogue imagination and let her hand go. 'We should leave, or we'll be late.'

He took her by the arm and led her out of the villa and into the passenger seat of his car.

Sasha took in the view of Athens as they came down from the hills and entered the ancient city. The view was helping to distract her from the proximity of Apollo's all too masculine presence beside her.

The city was bustling, full of young people out on the streets, enjoying the weekend, laughing and enjoying life. She could see the Acropolis standing majestically over the city, like a sentinel. 'Have I been to the Acropolis?' she asked, as the thought occurred to her.

Apollo glanced at her, slowing to a stop at a set of lights. 'No, you didn't express an interest in seeing it.'

Sasha frowned. It was so disconcerting that someone else knew more about her than she did. Before long, they were driving into a wide leafy street with tall exclusive townhouses, and then through huge wrought-iron gates manned by serious-looking security men. They pulled up outside what could only be described as a neo-classical mansion.

Lots of people were milling around outside, then slowly making their way inside. Women dressed in long glittering dresses, men dressed like Apollo, in tuxedoes.

Nerves erupted like butterflies in her belly. Again, she regretted ever saying anything about coming. But the car had stopped and Apollo was uncoiling his tall body out of the car and handing the keys to a young man.

Then he was opening her door and holding out a hand. She took a deep breath and let him help her out. Not even her awareness of him was able to eclipse her nerves. Her palms were clammy. She didn't belong in a place like this and she didn't need to regain her memory to know that.

CHAPTER FOUR

APOLLO'S HAND WAS on Sasha's elbow, guiding her through the throng. He noticed the looks from his peers. The widening eyes as they registered his wife by his side. He gritted his jaw. He'd never asked for this—to be married—but he'd been surprised at what a difference it had made. Much as he hated to admit it, Sasha had been right in her estimation of the worth of having a wife by your side.

It made his married colleagues less nervous. It kept predatory women at bay. And it had lent a more stable veneer to his business. A couple of business associates he'd been trying to meet with for years had finally agreed to meetings and Apollo had realised that it had been because they were family men and they hadn't totally trusted him when he'd been a bachelor. He'd been seen as a rogue operator.

He looked down at Sasha to check how she was reacting and saw her expression. Genuinely awed, as if she'd never been in this kind of environment before. Certainly not how she'd reacted the first time he'd brought her to an event. Then she'd looked as entitled as everyone else here. Or, at least, she'd tried to.

Now she wore the kind of expression that one would never see in a place like this because everyone was too used to this level of luxury, or wouldn't be caught dead admitting to being impressed. Or too cynical.

To his surprise, her reaction reminded him of how he'd felt when he'd first started being invited along to high society events: out of his depth and as if he didn't belong.

He quickly quashed the sense of empathy. Sasha had led him a merry dance for months now, and she owed him. She seemed determined to act the part of his wife again and he'd be an idiot not to take advantage of that. After all, they wouldn't be married for much longer— as soon as she had fully recuperated—

She interrupted his thoughts, asking, 'What *is* this place?'

'It's the French Ambassador's residence. He's hosting this evening. His wife died of cancer some years ago and now he and his family host this ball every year.'

'Oh, that's sad.'

Apollo looked at her suspiciously. But she seemed genuinely concerned. A little frown between her eyes. Mouth turned down.

Sasha was unaware of the speculative look from her husband. She was too consumed and awed by her surroundings. She'd never seen such glittering opulence. The ceilings had elaborate frescoes and the walls seemed to be made out of gold.

Hundreds of candles and sparkling chandeliers imbued everything with a golden glow. It truly was another world. She was sure she'd never seen so many beautiful people in one place. Or maybe she had, if she'd been serving them drinks. But not like this…not as one of them.

Frustration bit at her insides. She hated this…*not knowing*. Being at the mercy of her mind choosing to reveal memories totally at random. When *it* chose to. Like when she'd seen Apollo in the tuxedo.

To distract herself, Sasha tried to tune into the conversation Apollo was having with some men, but she gave up as it was in Greek, or other languages she didn't understand.

Waiters came around offering champagne and canapés. Sasha was too afraid to eat in case she ruined her dress. Then they were led into another large and impressive room with round tables set around a small stage. They sat down and a charity auction took place. The items up for auction included cars, date nights with famous celebrities and even a small island off the coast of Ireland.

Sasha gasped when that lot was announced. 'That's outrageous!'

Apollo looked at her and his mouth twisted slightly. 'That's the super-rich.'

Then a lot came up for a luxury yacht. To her shock and surprise, Apollo started bidding on it. Within a few short minutes people were clapping him on the back and cheering. He'd paid an extortionate amount of money for it.

Sasha was in shock. 'You just bought a yacht.'

He looked at her. 'Well, I already have an island and an island isn't much use without a yacht.'

He said that without any discernible sense of awe

that he owned such fantastical things. In fact, he almost sounded…bored.

'You don't seem very excited to own such things.'

Apollo felt something hitch in his chest at Sasha's comment and the way her blue eyes seemed to be looking right inside him, to the place where a sense of novelty had become something else. Something *less* novel. When had that happened?

He shrugged nonchalantly when he felt tight inside, not relaxed, 'Like I said, an island needs a yacht.'

'But will you use it?'

Apollo was surprised at the hollow feeling that seemed to spread outwards from his centre. He hadn't even consciously bought the yacht with a view to using it. More as a reflex to do what was expected of him. But now he couldn't help imagining the vessel bobbing in azure waters under a clear sky, and this woman laid out in all her slender, pale glory…red hair spread around her head—

The crowd seemed to stand en masse as the auction came to an end and Apollo seized the opportunity to divert Sasha's attention. Since when had his wife had the ability to probe so insightfully and deeply with just a casual question?

He stood up and reached for her hand. 'It's time to move on.'

Sasha had a very keen sense that Apollo hadn't appreciated her innocent questions. Clearly she'd hit on a nerve and maybe she was being spectacularly naive: in this world, islands and yachts were mere luxury trinkets to be added to a portfolio of even more luxury items.

There was just something about his lack of enthusiasm that struck at the heart of her, making her feel a little…sad.

The crowd was moving into yet another glorious room, even bigger. A ballroom. There was an orchestra and a singer singing sultry jazz songs. The lighting was dim and intimate. French doors were open, leading out to a terrace lined with flaming lanterns. Dusk was falling and the sky was a deep lavender colour. It was like a scene from a fairy-tale or a movie.

Her hand was still in Apollo's and she was very conscious of his long fingers wrapped around hers, so much so that she didn't even notice that he was leading her onto the dance floor. When she realised where they were, it was too late. He was drawing her in front of him and wrapping one arm across her back.

She went rigid in his arms from the impact of his body against hers as much because of where they were; in the middle of a dance floor. Around them, couples were moving sinuously to the music. Graceful and elegant. At ease.

Apollo started to move, taking Sasha with him, and she hissed, 'I don't even know if I can dance.'

'Just follow my lead.'

After a few robotic moments, Apollo pulled her even closer to his body. Sasha couldn't fight the force it took to remain rigid and so she softened against him.

She was surrounded by him, his steely strength. They were so close she could smell the sharp tang of his aftershave. Her heels put her even closer to his jaw and mouth. She wanted to press her lips there, taste his skin. Immediately she tensed again and he lowered his head, saying in her ear, 'Relax. Just let me lead.'

After a few torturous seconds she allowed herself to soften again. She realised they were moving around the floor with relative grace. She looked up, avoiding looking at his jaw and the faint line of stubble.

'Where did you learn to dance?'

She felt the tension come into his body. 'My mother. She loved to dance, she used to dance with my father all the time.'

'That's romantic.'

He looked down at her, his expression anything but romantic. 'It was, until he had the accident and couldn't dance any more.'

Sasha thought of what he'd told her about getting revenge for his father's death. She shivered slightly, thinking of how ruthless he must have been. Single-minded. But she remembered him being like that with her—until she'd agreed to go for a drink with him.

She wondered how on earth she'd caught his eye in London when they'd been surrounded by women as beautiful as the ones here tonight, in their peacock dresses and glittering jewels. Even though she was dressed like them now, she felt dowdy and colourless in comparison.

She noticed one dark brunette pass by in the arms of her partner, her voluptuous body poured into a silver sheath dress. She also noticed how she looked at Apollo, and then at Sasha, dismissing her with a flick of her hair. No competition.

The song came to an end and Sasha seized the opportunity to escape for a moment, hating this feeling of insecurity. Especially when she thought of how close she'd come last night to showing Apollo how much he affected her. When he clearly felt nothing similar. She pulled back from Apollo's arms. 'Excuse me, I just need to go to the bathroom.'

Apollo watched Sasha hurry from the dance floor. Her face had been the colour of milk. He couldn't stop the spike of concern. Was she feeling ill? Was it her memory? Was she remembering more?

He cursed and made his way over to the bar. Concern for his wife was a novel and unwelcome sentiment. Also unwelcome was the raging arousal still lingering in his blood after that dance. Holding her so close, smelling her scent. The thin fabric of her dress doing little to hide how her slender curves had felt against his body... no other woman had ever had such an effect on him.

He took women he desired to bed. He told them up front that he wasn't looking for anything permanent. Except *her*. Everything about his experience with her had been so novel, and that's why he'd let his guard down momentarily. A moment she'd exploited when she'd come to him in London a month after their night together with her shock announcement.

But all of that was in danger of being forgotten with the rush of hot desire in his blood. Clouding his judgement. Blunting his control. Changing things. He should never have agreed to let her join him tonight. They weren't a couple.

They never would have married if it hadn't been for—

Apollo saw Sasha return to the room. Her head was turning left and right, clearly searching for him.

She looked vulnerable. Out of place. He saw more than one man look at her twice, caught by her fresh-faced beauty. She stood out in a crowd of rich and jaded cynics. And that's why she'd appealed to him that very first night.

But it had all been a mirage. Her memory loss might very well be real, but underneath it lay the true Sasha Miller. A liar and a mercenary bitch. It wouldn't be long before she showed her true colours again. At that moment, as if hearing his thoughts, she saw him and their eyes locked across the room. Apollo vowed not to forget who she really was.

The journey winding back up the hills to Apollo's villa was taken in silence. Sasha was engrossed in her own thoughts. The questions buzzing in her brain were growing increasingly loud and hard to ignore. Especially after tonight when she'd gone out in public, pretending to the world that she was this man's wife. When reality couldn't be further from that truth.

Apollo parked the car at the foot of the steps leading up to the front door of the villa. Sasha turned to him in the gloom of the car. 'Why did you let me come with you tonight?'

Apollo put his hands on the wheel. 'Primarily because I didn't expect you to be ready on time. You never were before.'

'So that would have been your excuse for leaving me behind.'

He looked at her and shrugged minutely, unapologetic.

Sasha shook her head. 'What happened, Apollo? Why are we like this? You liked me in London. You pursued me...asked me for a drink. Took me for dinner.'

Took me to bed?

She couldn't remember those details but she sensed *yes*, because her body was attuned to his on a level that she couldn't deny. And would a man like Apollo have married her without sleeping with her? He didn't strike her as the traditional type.

Was she? Had she been a virgin?

'You really want to get into this now?'

Once again she wasn't sure. Did she want to know everything? But she heard herself say, 'Yes.'

'Are you sure you're ready?'

Sasha swallowed the rising fear. 'I need to know. I feel like I'm the only one left out of a secret.'

'Very well. But not here—inside.'

A feeling of panic eclipsed the fear as Sasha followed Apollo inside the villa. Was she really ready for this? *No.* But she knew she couldn't continue not knowing either.

It was quiet. The staff had gone home or were in bed. He led the way into one of the less formal drawing rooms, flicking on low lights.

He went over to a drinks cabinet, tugging at the bowtie around his neck. He looked back at her, 'Would you like a drink?'

'Will I need one?' Sasha joked, but it felt hollow.

He arched a brow and she said, 'A small brandy, please.' She wasn't even sure if she'd ever had brandy before but felt like it might be necessary.

Apollo poured a drink for himself and brought her over a small tumbler. She took a sniff and wrinkled her nose at the strong smell. She took a tentative sip and the liquid slid down her throat and into her stomach, leaving a trail of fire and a lingering afterglow of heat. It wasn't unpleasant.

Apollo shrugged off his jacket and Sasha wished he hadn't because now she could see the play of muscles under the thin material of his shirt. He faced her. 'What do you want to know?

Everything.

She swallowed. Where to start? 'Did we sleep together?'

'Yes. We spent one night together.'

An instant flush of heat landed in Sasha's belly that had nothing to do with the alcohol. Her instinct had been right. She'd slept with this man.

That was why her body remembered.

But she didn't.

She swallowed. 'The night we had dinner in... The Shard?'

He nodded. 'Yes, then you came back to my apartment.'

Ridiculously she almost felt like apologising for not being able to remember. Instinctively she felt that it had been memorable, and that a man like Apollo wasn't easily forgotten.

Her hand gripped the glass. 'Was I...? Was it my first time?'

His jaw clenched. 'I believed it was, yes. But since then...let's just say that I can't be sure you didn't make it seem that way.'

Sasha felt something like shame creep up inside her. 'Why would I lie about being a virgin?'

He looked at her and she couldn't escape that green gaze or the clear admonishment. 'To make yourself appear more innocent than you were. Because you thought it would appeal to me, a jaded cynic? Who knows?'

'I didn't tell you beforehand?'

He shook his head. 'You said you were afraid that if I'd known how inexperienced you were, I wouldn't want you.'

Sasha sat down on a seat behind her, her legs feeling distinctly wobbly.

'What happened then?'

Apollo drank the contents of his glass and put it down carefully. He faced her and folded his arms across his chest. He looked like a warrior, preparing for battle. All sinew and muscle. Not an inch of softness.

'After that night we went our separate ways.'

Sasha absorbed that. Had it been a mutual decision? She shied away from asking that question now. It was enough to absorb that he'd been her first lover.

Or had he?

She felt an instinctive need to reject his claim that she might not have been innocent. But how could she defend herself when she didn't know for sure?

She took another sip of the fiery drink, her hand not quite steady. 'If we went our separate ways…then how… did we end up here, married?'

For a second her heart palpitated. Maybe he'd come after her? Maybe one night hadn't been enough?

He paused for a moment and then he said, 'Because a month after that night, you came to my offices in London and you told me that you were pregnant with my child.'

Sasha stood up slowly, there was a roaring sound in

her ears and she had to shake her head to clear it. 'I'm sorry… I what?'

He spoke slowly. 'You told me that you were pregnant with my child.'

CHAPTER FIVE

THE WORD SANK into Sasha's head but didn't make sense. *Pregnant.* She put a hand to her belly but it was flat. Something occurred to her and she felt her blood drain south. The glass fell out of nerveless fingers but she barely noticed Apollo stride forward to pick it up and take her arm, pushing her gently back into the chair.

She looked up at him. 'Did I lose it?'

How could she not know if she'd lost her own baby? Was that why Apollo hated her? For losing their baby?

Both hands were on her belly now as if that could help her to remember something so huge…so cataclysmic.

But Apollo was shaking his head. 'No. You didn't lose it, because you were never pregnant in the first place. You deliberately lied about being pregnant to get me to marry you, Sasha.'

She hadn't been pregnant.

In the midst of the relief that she hadn't forgotten such a seismic event, Apollo's words sank in.

'You deliberately lied. To get me to marry you.'

Sasha's first reaction was denial. Rejection. She

shook her head. 'No... I wouldn't have said that. I couldn't have done something like that...'

'But you did,' Apollo countered curtly.

She was glad she was sitting down because she was pretty sure she would have collapsed otherwise. 'I... I told you I was pregnant. But I wasn't?'

He nodded. His face was impossibly grim.

She tried to make sense of it all, and also the gut-wrenching knowledge that he *hadn't* come after her, because she'd been the one to go to him in the end. 'But why would I do such a thing?'

His mouth went thin. 'You really have to ask that question? We slept together and you saw an opportunity.'

He indicated with a hand. 'Look around you. You hungered for a better life and you were going to use me to get it.'

A moment ago Sasha had felt as if her legs wouldn't support her but now she stood again, too agitated to keep sitting. She paced back and forth. 'But that's...' She stopped. 'That's an awful thing to do.'

'Yes, it is,' he agreed.

She struggled to recall any hint of what might have led her to do such a drastic thing but her mind stayed annoyingly blank.

'Maybe I believed I was pregnant? Did we...use protection?'

His whole body bristled. 'Of course. I would never be so lax. But I will admit that I didn't check afterwards. There's always a possibility of failure and you capitalised on that, sowing the seed of doubt in my mind.'

'But how were you so sure I'd lied about the pregnancy?'

'I had my suspicions when you showed no signs of pregnancy and then after an…incident you admitted it was a lie.'

'An incident…?'

He nodded and paced away from her, turned back. 'I was in London on business and came back after a panicked call from Rhea. You were hosting a party with some new-found friends.'

The way Apollo's lip curled on *friends* told her what he'd thought of them. 'I found you snorting cocaine and drinking. When you'd sobered up you admitted it had been a lie to trap me.'

Sasha went back to the chair and sat down again. Reeling. She felt cold and wrapped her arms around herself.

She forced herself to look at Apollo. She felt deep in her bones that she wouldn't have done such heinous things—lying about being pregnant, taking drugs—*couldn't* have. And yet why would he lie? This explained his antipathy and also the way Rhea and Kara had looked at her like an unexploded bomb on her return from the hospital.

She went even colder as she absorbed the full extent of everything he'd told her. 'You didn't want to marry me.'

His jaw tightened. 'No.' Just that. *No.*

Why not? trembled on her lips but she didn't have to ask that question. He hadn't been interested in her after their night together in London. Her innocence must have been a huge turn-off.

Desperately trying to salvage something positive, she said, 'But in London you took me for dinner…to your apartment… You liked me then?' She hated how insecure she sounded.

A sense of exposure hit Apollo again. His voice was taut with self-recrimination. 'You captivated me. Briefly. You were different.'

'Different from what?'

Sasha looked so guileless. Pale. Eyes huge.

Was she really faking this amnesia? Was it too convenient that she was remembering snippets but not everything? Was she laughing at him? Forcing him to articulate why he'd wanted her?

But something uneasy in his gut told him that she couldn't be faking it. She looked too tortured.

He said, 'Different from everyone else. Other women.'

Twin flags of pink made her cheeks flush and for a moment Apollo was rewarded with a flashback to watching her face flush with pleasure as she'd moved under him, around him.

She said tightly, 'You mean I wasn't as sophisticated.'

Apollo had to use every atom of his control to counter the rush of desire. Damn her. 'You caught my eye. You were refreshingly unaffected. Open. Friendly. But it was all a lie.'

Sasha remembered feeling invisible that night. Until he'd looked directly at her, and the flash of pure heat that had gone through her body. Her tray of drinks had wobbled precariously and he'd stepped forward and steadied it. His lazy, charming smile.

'Promise to meet me for a drink and I'll give the tray back.'

She couldn't remember sleeping with him or the aftermath, but she could imagine all too easily how he would have laid it out. Telling her not to expect more. A man like this would have been used to such scenarios with women. Had she been so desperate that she'd begged for more? She felt ashamed for herself.

In a way now Sasha was glad she couldn't remember exactly what had happened. This was humiliating enough without recalling in excruciating detail how banal the experience must have been for a man of the world like him. To sleep with a virgin. She'd obviously been a novelty for a jaded billionaire and her appeal hadn't lasted long.

Her head was starting to throb faintly. 'What happens now?'

'Nothing. Until you've recovered fully. Then we can discuss the future.'

The future.

Sasha felt slightly hysterical. She couldn't recall much of the past, never mind the future.

She stood up. 'I'm getting a headache. I think I'll go to bed.'

Apollo watched as she turned and walked out. She was the colour of pale parchment. Maybe it had been too soon to tell her the unvarnished truth? No matter how much she'd insisted she wanted to know.

He felt an impulse to go after her and make sure she was okay but he told himself he was being ridiculous. The woman who had engineered a fake pregnancy to trap him into marriage was no delicate soul. Accident or no accident.

He poured himself another shot of whisky and downed it in one. It burned his throat. But he couldn't get her pale face and huge shocked eyes out of his mind. He had to admit that he was finding it hard to continue suspecting that she was faking the amnesia. Sasha would never have been able to play this far more innocent incarnation for so long without cracking.

Which meant…this news was as shocking to her now as it had been to him when he'd first heard it.

Apollo cursed and put down the glass. He went upstairs and stood outside Sasha's bedroom door for a long moment. He heard no sounds.

He knocked lightly but again there was no sound. He opened the door and went in. His eyes took a moment to adjust to the dim light. He could see no shape in the bed. And then he saw her, standing outside on the balcony.

She must have heard him because she turned around. She'd changed. She was wearing a diaphanous robe over what looked like a short negligée. From where he stood, Apollo could see the outline of her body. All slender curves and pale skin.

His blood surged, and he realised in that moment that he shouldn't have come up here. Sasha stepped into the room. 'Is something wrong?'

But instead of leaving, Apollo moved towards her as if drawn by a magnet. The moon was behind her, low in the sky. A perfect crescent. The milky glow made her look ethereal, adding a silver tinge to her rose-gold hair. It was down again, falling in soft waves over her shoulders.

He had an urge to touch her to make sure she was, in fact, real. He stopped a couple of feet away. Her scent reached him—lemon, underlain with something more tantalisingly exotic. But soft, not overpowering.

Different.

'You said you had a headache.'

She touched her head. 'It's okay now, thank you. I think it was just taking in all that information...'

Sasha wasn't sure that she wasn't hallucinating right now. Was Apollo really standing in her room, looking at her as if he'd never seen her before?

But then, at that moment, he said, 'I just wanted to check you were okay,' and then turned around as if to leave.

Sasha acted on an impulse, reaching out with her hand. 'Wait.'

He stopped. Turned around. Sasha wasn't even sure what she wanted to say. And then she did. She dropped her outstretched hand. 'I don't remember anything of what you said... It doesn't feel like something I would do but then how do I know?'

She bit her lip. 'Did you even care about the baby?'

Apollo had to school his expression in case she saw something he didn't want to reveal. The pain of losing his entire family over a period of a few years had been so acute that he'd always vowed to avoid such pain again by not having a family of his own.

But, to his surprise, after the initial shock and anger at Sasha's pregnancy news had abated, he'd found that the thought of a baby he could protect and nurture had softened something inside him. And had restored a broken sense of hope, optimism.

But then, the fact that she'd lied about it and roused those feelings had made a cruel mockery of the defences he'd built up over the years. They hadn't been strong after all. Now, though, they were ironclad. Not that he would ever reveal to her what she'd done to him. She'd revealed a weakness, and reopened a wound and he would never forgive her for that.

'I had never intended on having a relationship or becoming a father. Not after losing my entire family. But of course I would have cared for any child of mine. I'm not a monster.'

Sasha's eyes were huge. Full of emotion. Exposure prickled over his skin just as she said huskily, 'I'm sorry…for what happened. I don't know why I pretended to be pregnant but I'd like to think I had good reasons.'

He fought against the image she was projecting of someone compassionate, who *cared*. He should move back, out of her dangerous orbit, but instead he found himself moving closer. All he could see was her. Looking impossibly innocent. Impossibly because she hadn't been innocent at all. Or had she? Physically perhaps, at least.

He had an intensely erotic memory of how it had felt to thrust deep into that silken embrace. Her muscles had clamped so tightly around him he'd seen stars.

Angry at his lack of control, he asked curtly, 'Are you really sorry, though? Or is this just an elaborate showcase of your acting skills to entice me back into your bed so you can try to get pregnant for real?'

Horror at his relentless cynicism made Sasha take a step back. '*No.* How can you say such a thing?'

Apollo's mouth was a thin line. 'Very easily, because you did it before, countless times, including the memorable occasion when I came home to find you naked in my bed.'

Shock and disbelief made Sasha take another step back. She shook her head. 'No, there is no way I would have ever done such a thing.'

Apollo just arched a brow. 'Why would I lie? You have to agree it made sense. After all, you weren't pregnant so you needed to get pregnant. Fast.'

Sasha swallowed. Had that really been her? So desperate? Conniving? She struggled to defend herself when she felt as if everything inside her was crumbling. 'But it's obvious you don't want me—why would I have humiliated myself like that?'

Apollo was looking at her so intensely she could scarcely breathe.

He said something under his breath then, a word she didn't understand, and then said, almost as if to himself, 'I thought I didn't want you any more, but now it's all I can think about. What kind of sorcery is this?'

Sasha's heart slammed to a stop, and then started again in an erratic rhythm. She suddenly became very aware of her flimsy garments. The silky thigh-skimming negligée and floaty dressing gown. Garments she didn't feel particularly comfortable in, but apparently she hadn't favoured comfort over style.

She tried to speak. 'I don't… There's no sorcery.'

His gaze raked her up and down and she trembled under its force. Her breasts felt heavy, their tips tightening into hard points, pressing against the silky material. Her body remembered this man. His touch. But she didn't. Frustration coursed through her. She couldn't take her eyes off his mouth, the firm sculpted lines.

Apollo barely heard Sasha's denial. He knew this was madness. That he shouldn't have come to her bedroom. But rational thought was fast dissolving in a haze of lust. He reached out and caught a loose tendril of silky hair, winding it around his finger, tugging her gently towards him.

When he looked down he could see her breasts rising and falling with her rapid breath, pale swells framed enticingly by lace, inviting him to touch, explore. Electricity hummed between them, thick and urgent.

He tipped her chin up with his forefinger and thumb. Her eyes were huge pools of blue. He had a flashback to the first time he'd kissed her, sitting in a discreet booth of the exclusive hotel bar where he'd taken her for a drink when she'd finished work on that first night.

It had been a rare novelty, waiting for her to emerge from a staff entrance of the hotel. He could remember the sensation of something loosening inside him. He'd been so focused for so long and suddenly he'd been diverted from that single-mindedness.

She'd been endearingly self-conscious in her black skirt, white shirt and black jacket. Flat shoes. Sheer tights.

He'd wanted her then and he wanted her now. He lowered his head, anticipation prickling across his skin. He'd thought he'd never kiss her again.

Hadn't wanted to.

But he was being punished for that complacency now, because here he was, as consumed with lust as he had been the first time.

* * *

Tension was a tight coil inside Sasha as she waited for Apollo's mouth to touch hers and she told herself desperately that he'd kissed her before—more than kissed her, so it shouldn't come as a shock—but when his mouth touched hers, it was more than a shock. It was an earthquake, erupting from her solar plexus and spreading out to every nerve-ending, bringing with it thousands of volts of electricity.

She wasn't even aware of her hands going to his shirt and clinging on for dear life. His hands were in her hair, angling her head, and their mouths were on fire. She tasted the whisky he'd been drinking and she felt molten and solid all at the same time. It was intoxicating, and nothing could have prepared her for this.

His chest was a steel wall against her breasts. She arched instinctively closer, seeking closer contact. One of his hands moved down, skimming over her arm, around to her back, pressing her even closer.

His arousal pressed against her lower belly and the flood of damp heat between her legs was almost embarrassing. She pressed her thighs together in a bid to stem the rising tide of desire but it was impossible.

But at that very moment Apollo pulled back. It was so sudden that Sasha went with him and he had to steady her, putting his hands on her arms. She opened her eyes, feeling dizzy. Stunned.

She was breathing as if she'd run a race. Her heart was hammering, and a hunger that was new and yet familiar at the same time pounded through her blood, demanding to be satisfied. She felt greedy. *Needy.*

It took a second for Apollo's face to come back into

focus and when she registered his harsh expression she pulled free of his hands, even though her legs still felt jittery.

He said, 'That shouldn't have happened. It was never part of this marriage deal. Go to bed, Sasha, it's late.'

He turned and left the room and Sasha stared after the empty space for a long minute. She felt too shell-shocked to even be irritated that he'd spoken to her like a child, as if she'd walked into *his* room and kissed *him*.

Her skin felt seared alive, her heart was still racing and her whole body was crying out for a fulfilment it knew but couldn't remember. Her breasts ached and she throbbed between her legs, and that was after just a kiss.

She moved on autopilot, closing the doors to the balcony, slipping out of the robe and under the covers of the bed. She eventually fell into a fitful sleep, with thoughts and dreams full of disjointed, disturbing images.

Apollo stood under the punishing spray of a cold shower for longer than he could almost bear. Eventually he got out and hitched a towel around his waist, catching his reflection in the mirror above the sink.

He looked pained. And he knew it wasn't from the cold shower. What the hell had he been thinking—going to Sasha's room? Kissing her? He hadn't been thinking. That was the problem.

It had taken every ounce of his restraint to pull back and not rip apart those flimsy garments, spreading her back on the bed so he could relive the night they'd shared in London. So that he could consummate this marriage.

This marriage was not about consummation or sleeping together. And while he hadn't wanted her it had been all too easy to forget he had ever wanted her.

You never forgot.

He scowled at his reflection.

But now the floodgates were open. He'd tasted Sasha again and she was as potent as she had been the first time.

He wanted his wife.

But she was the last thing he should want. Especially not when she had the ability to reopen old wounds with just a look from those huge eyes. What he needed was to excise Sasha from his life once and for all.

And for that to happen she needed to regain her memory. The sooner that happened and she reverted to her duplicitous nature, the sooner Apollo could get on with his life and forget she'd ever existed.

What he needed to do now was provide every opportunity to nudge her memory in the right direction.

Sasha was trying to avoid looking at Apollo across the breakfast table on the outdoor terrace. She was still raw after that kiss and gritty-eyed after a mostly sleepless night, broken by disturbing dreams she was afraid to analyse.

The impulse to look, though, was too strong and she glanced his way to see him lifting a small coffee cup to his mouth, his gaze on the paper in his hand. To her intense irritation he looked as if nothing had happened last night. He was as cool and fresh as if he'd enjoyed the sleep of a baby.

He was clean-shaven and the memory of his stubble against her jaw made heat rise up through her body. For a breathless panicky moment she wondered if she'd, in fact, dreamt that kiss, but then he put his paper down and looked at her and the jolt of electricity that went straight to her solar plexus told her that kiss at least hadn't been a dream. It was of little comfort.

'We're going to go to Krisakis for a few days.'

She forced her brain to function. 'Kris— Where?'

'It's the island I own. It's part of the Cyclades chain of islands. Santorini, Naxos, Paros…'

She'd forgotten that he owned an island.

'I'm constructing an eco-resort and I need to check progress and meet with some of the designers.'

'Have I been there before?'

He nodded. 'I took you there when we first came to Greece.'

Sasha tried to conjure up an image of what the island might be like but her mind stubbornly refused to provide anything.

Right at that moment, after the dreams she'd had last night, she relished the thought of a change of scenery. 'When do we leave?'

Apollo looked at his watch. 'In an hour. I've instructed Kara to pack some things for you.'

She felt prickly. 'I can pack my own bag.'

Apollo shrugged. 'As you wish. I need to make some calls before we go.' He got up and walked out of the room and Sasha's breath got stuck in her throat as she watched him go. He was wearing a polo shirt and faded jeans that lovingly hugged his buttocks and thighs.

Rhea bustled into the room and Sasha looked away quickly, mortified to have been caught ogling her husband, but also when she recalled what Apollo had told her about the party she'd hosted.

Taking drugs.

Her conscience wouldn't let her say nothing, though, and she caught Rhea's hand before she could clear the plates. The woman looked at her warily. Sasha said, 'I'm so sorry, Rhea…for what happened. For disrespecting you and this house.'

The older woman's expression softened. She patted Sasha's hand awkwardly. 'Is okay, Kyria Vasilis. Don't worry.'

She cleared the plates efficiently and left the room. Sasha still felt humiliated but a little lighter.

She stood up to leave the table and on an impulse walked down through the gardens. In spite of the sun, tentacles of those disturbing dreams from last night lingered, making her shiver a little.

The dreams had been shockingly erotic. She'd been on a bed, making love to Apollo. Their naked bodies entwined in the most intimate way possible. He'd held one of her hands over her head, capturing it, and his head had moved down, over her body, his mouth fastening over one nipple, feasting on her tender flesh. She could still feel it now, the delicious pulling, dragging sensation that had gone all the way down to between her legs where he'd pushed them apart with his thigh, opening her up to his body…

But then, abruptly, Sasha had realised that she was no longer in the body on the bed; she was standing apart, looking at him making love to another woman. Not her. But then the woman's face had been revealed and she'd smiled mockingly at Sasha and Sasha had realised that it *was* her. But it wasn't her.

She'd been separated from them by a glass wall. Able to see everything but not feel it. The woman on the bed was an imposter, pretending to be her. And Apollo didn't realise. She'd watched helplessly as he'd moved his powerful body between the woman's legs, how she'd opened up for him, and then the moment when he'd thrust deep inside.

The woman's legs were wrapped around Apollo's waist and the whole time she'd looked at Sasha and then her mocking smile had turned to nightmarish laughter and that's when Sasha had woken, sweating and trembling from the force of it, filled with a feeling of doom and betrayal so acrid that she'd felt nauseous.

Sasha shook her head to try and dislodge the images and that horrible feeling of betrayal. But it had felt so real. And it couldn't be, obviously.

She went back inside, but on her way to the bedroom she passed by her office. She could hear the deep tones of Apollo's voice through his own office door.

On an impulse she went into the white and fluffy room, still a bit bemused at the thought that she'd insisted on having an office. There was a computer on the desk and she sat down and tapped a key experimentally. It opened automatically in an internet browser.

Wondering how it hadn't occurred to her before, she put Apollo's name into the search engine. The first items to pop up were recent deals and headlines like *Vasilis and His Midas Touch Strike Again!*

Sasha skimmed a recent profile article done for a prominent British financial newspaper where it talked about Apollo's myriad achievements and rapid rise to stratospheric success. He was also one of the first construction titans to commit to working ethically. Every worker on one of his sites had proper healthcare and insurance and if accidents occurred, workers were rehabilitated and then redeployed either back to where they'd been or to a new area more suited to them.

Consequently, his workers were among the happiest in a normally fickle industry and by holding himself to a higher standard, he was forcing the industry to change around him. He was a trailblazer.

At the end of the article it said:

When asked about his recent marriage to Sasha Miller, Vasilis was curt, saying, 'My private life is off-limits.'

Sasha felt sick. Unsurprisingly he hadn't wanted to divulge the details of his marriage of inconvenience to an interviewer.

It only made Sasha want to know more about her own past—what had happened to her to make her behave like that? To trap a man into marriage? She went back into the history of the computer and saw some social media account tabs and clicked on them. But they'd all been logged out and she couldn't remember the passwords.

For one of the main social accounts she could see a small picture of herself, smiling widely against a glamorous-looking backdrop of a marina. She was wearing more make-up. Her skin was tanned...which must have been fake because she was naturally the colour of a milk bottle. She was holding up a glass of sparkling wine. It sparkled almost as much as the massive diamond on her ring finger. It eclipsed the much plainer gold wedding band. The rings that had gone missing in the accident.

She rubbed her finger absently, imagining them being torn off somehow, but there was no mark on her finger or bruising to indicate what had happened. Something about that niggled at the edges of her memory. A sense that she had seen them somewhere…but not on her hand. But the memory refused to be pinned down. Again.

Sasha touched the picture of her face with a finger, as if that could unlock the secrets of her past.

Nothing.

Nothing except a tiny shiver down her spine. Looking at her face like this reminded her of that dream, because it was like looking at another person.

She turned off the computer, eager to put that image of her face, and the dream, behind her. She saw a drawer in the desk and opened it, vaguely wondering if she might find some other clues to her past.

There was a thick manila envelope inside and she pulled it out. It had her name on it. For some reason, she felt superstitious about looking at the contents but the envelope was open and it was addressed to her.

She pulled out a thick sheaf of papers and read the words at the top of the first page: 'Application For Mutual Consent Divorce Proceedings Between Apollo Vasilis and Sasha Miller'.

It was dated a few days before the accident.

Sasha started to look through the pages, which weren't signed yet. They outlined the grounds for divorce. Irreconcilable differences. And non-consummation of the marriage.

They hadn't slept together.

So he really hadn't wanted her. But last night...he had. And he hadn't welcomed it.

'What are you doing?'

Sasha looked up to see Apollo standing in the doorway. She was too shocked to be embarrassed or feel like he'd caught her doing something illicit.

She held up the document. 'We were going to divorce?'

'We were always going to divorce.'

Sasha dropped the document back on the desk. 'But what about at first...when the baby...?' She trailed off, realising what she was saying.

He arched a brow, 'The baby that never existed?'

She flushed guiltily.

'When I believed you were pregnant we agreed to marry for a year, enough time to have the baby and then reassess the situation.'

Sasha frowned. 'What does that mean?'

'Custody.'

She struggled to understand. 'But presumably as the mother I would have had custody.'

Apollo shook his head. 'In the pre-nuptial agreement you signed away your right to full custody. You agreed to an arrangement where I would have full custody and I would set you up somewhere close enough for you to see the child on a regular basis.'

Sasha stood up. She shook her head. 'I can't believe I would have signed away full rights to my own baby.'

Apollo's lip curled. 'Don't forget there *was* no baby.

I should have guessed something was amiss when you agreed so quickly to that, and when you were more interested in the alimony you would receive in the event of a divorce.'

Sasha remembered what he'd told her last night about how she'd tried to seduce him. To try and get pregnant. She felt sick. And even sicker when she thought of how he'd found her in such a debauched state. Taking drugs.

She forced herself to look at him. 'That's when you initiated the divorce, after the party, when you knew I wasn't pregnant.'

He nodded.

'Why didn't you just throw me out, once you knew?' She would have thrown her out. She felt angry at *herself.*

'I considered it. I wanted to. I never wanted to see you again. You disgusted me.'

Sasha felt every word like a little sharp knife to her heart. 'So why didn't you?'

'Because we are married. I couldn't trust you. I didn't know what you would do. You could have gone to the papers with some sob story and I have a reputation to maintain. The last thing I needed was adverse press attention.'

'And then I had the accident.'

He nodded. 'A few days later, you took one of the cars and disappeared for hours. When you hadn't returned by dinner-time, Rhea called me and a search was started. You eventually appeared by the side of a road not far from here, further up into the hills.'

Sasha felt cold. 'This marriage never had a chance.'

Apollo faltered for a moment when he thought of that first night he'd met Sasha. How easily she'd caught him with her fresh-faced beauty. How novel it had been to meet someone unjaded. Open. Joyful. But it hadn't been real. He forced the memory out. 'No.'

Sasha looked bewildered. 'Why did you agree to marry me at all? Why did you believe me?'

Feeling almost defensive now, he said, 'You had a note from a doctor confirming the pregnancy. And I consulted my legal team. We came to the conclusion that once you agreed to sign a pre-nuptial agreement, marrying you would offer me the best chance of custody and securing my child's future. There was a clause to say that if anything happened to the pregnancy or if the baby proved not to be mine after a DNA test, you would get nothing. Obviously you'd decided that the risk of marriage was worth it, even though you weren't pregnant. Hence your attempts to try and seduce me once we were married. Attempts that didn't work.'

Sasha winced at that. 'Why did you bring me back here after the accident? Why not just kick me out of your life for good now that you can?'

Why not indeed? mocked a little voice in Apollo's head. He could have done exactly that. He could have taken advantage of her amnesia to get her to sign the divorce papers and set her up in an apartment in Athens with a small allowance and a nurse to attend to her needs until the divorce was through.

But no matter how much he'd hated her for what she'd done, the way she'd looked after the accident—so pale and defenceless on that hospital bed—it had caught at him. And then she'd woken up and looked at him and it had been as if the previous months had fallen away and all he could remember was that night they'd met.

Her memory loss had only complicated things further. Changing her. Reminding him of that first impression she'd made. Re-igniting his desire.

He said now, 'I'm not letting you go anywhere until we sign the divorce papers. I don't trust that you won't do something to exploit the power you have as my wife.'

He went on, 'I don't know why you took the car on the day you disappeared or where you went to…and until you regain your memory and you can tell me, you won't be going anywhere. For all I know, you took your wedding rings off because you have a lover, perhaps someone you were hoping to turn to because I hadn't fallen under your spell.'

A memory of that kiss last night blasted into Apollo's head, mocking him. He was under her spell again whether he liked it or not.

Sasha held up the sheaf of papers. She was pale. They were trembling lightly in her hand and that evidence of her emotions caught at him, making him feel an urge to protect her. He rejected it.

She said, 'So why don't we just sign the papers now and be done with it?'

To his disgust, his immediate emotion wasn't one of relief that she was showing a willingness to put all this behind them and get out of his life. It was something much more ambiguous and disturbing. Reluctance to let her go.

He said, 'It's the weekend, my offices won't be open. And next Monday is a national holiday. In any case I've made plans to go and inspect the site on Krisakis. We will stick to this arrangement and sign the papers when we return to Athens in a week. We'll be out of each other's lives within a month. And perhaps Krisakis will help jog your memory.'

Sasha felt winded. 'Once we sign the papers, it can happen that quickly?' The thought of never seeing Apollo again made her feel panicky. She told herself it was because he was the only familiar thing in her life, not because he'd come to mean anything to her. Clearly there had been little love lost between them.

Apollo's mouth firmed. 'Yes, it can happen that quickly. But obviously if your memory still hasn't returned by then, I'll make sure you're set up in a situation and place that feels secure and safe for you.'

Sasha wanted to curl inwards. The thought of Apollo pitying her enough to have to keep an eye on her after their marriage was over was a whole new level of humiliation.

'I'm sure that won't be necessary, but thank you.'

CHAPTER SIX

A COUPLE OF hours later, Apollo's words still reverberated in Sasha's head.

'I'll make sure you're set up in a situation and place that feels secure and safe for you.'

The perks of a rich man. Able to dissolve marriages and set up inconvenient ex-wives with a minimum of fuss.

The fact that the imminent dissolution of a marriage she'd apparently engineered into being through lies and deceit wasn't filling her with a sense of relief, only brought about more confusion.

She could remember being stunned by Apollo's interest in her when they'd first met. Intimidated but excited too. How had she gone from that to wanting to deceive him so heinously?

With a sigh, she let the landscape beneath her distract her from circling thoughts that were going nowhere and not helping.

They were in a helicopter, flying over the Aegean, and she looked down in awe at boats and islands that looked like toys beneath them.

When she'd seen the sleek black machine at the private airfield, she'd balked. Apollo had looked at her. 'You flew in this when I took you to the island the first time. You loved it.'

'Did I? Sasha had asked doubtfully. For the whole journey, in spite of her tortured thoughts and the beauty below them, her heart had been in her throat. And even more now as they started descending over an island and the helicopter tipped perilously to the left.

This must be Krisakis. Sasha forced down the fluttering panic and took in the rocky coastline where pockets of brightly coloured flowers flourished along the cliffs. The sea lapped against rocks and then they rounded a headland and an empty white sand beach appeared, like something on a postcard.

Sasha could see steps cut into the rocks, leading up to lush grounds and then up further to a white modern building—a series of buildings laid out like interconnecting cubes. Sunlight glinted off acres of glass. An infinity pool with sun loungers had never looked so inviting.

Apollo was saying into her headset, 'This is the villa, the first thing I built here. The island was hit by an earthquake about half a century ago, leaving only a small population behind. With the development I'm building on the other side of the island, it's becoming a thriving community again. People who were born here but who had to leave have returned to live out their last days, bringing their sons and daughters with them to make new lives.'

Sasha couldn't help thinking it was ironic for a man who'd professed little interest in having a family to be invested in bringing them together like this.

The helicopter was landing now on a helipad a little distance from the villa. When the pilot had touched down, Apollo got out. He opened Sasha's door and helped her out. Her legs felt like rubber and Apollo's hand tightened on hers. 'Okay?'

She locked her knees to stop them wobbling. 'Yes, fine.' She took her hand back.

Apollo stepped aside to talk to the pilot for a moment and then once the bags were unloaded he led her over to a safe spot while the helicopter lifted back up into the air before tilting to the right and heading off into the azure-blue sky.

Sasha put the sun hat she'd carried on her head, glad of Kara's thoughtfulness. Which was even more thoughtful now considering what she'd put them through. Sasha heard a faint sound and turned around to see what looked like a golf cart bouncing across the grounds towards them.

Apollo waved at the person driving who waved back enthusiastically. He said, 'That's Spiro—he's the son of my housekeeper here, helping out before he goes back to college.'

The young man jumped out when he'd come to a stop beside him, a big grin directed at Apollo as he took the bags, stowing them in the back.

Sasha couldn't help smiling at his cheerful effervescence but when he looked at her his smile faltered. Sasha's insides plummeted. Not again. Had she been rude to him too? The young man's eyes grew round and he said something to Apollo, who said something sharp back.

He held out his hand. 'Kyria Vasilis, nice to meet you again.'

Sasha forced a smile and took his hand, mentally apologising for whatever she'd done.

By the time they reached the stunning villa, she was preparing herself for the same reaction as she'd got from Kara and Rhea when she'd returned to the villa in Athens. Sure enough, Spiro's mother, Olympia, looked wary but kindly. Maybe Sasha hadn't behaved too badly on the island. After all, it didn't seem as if there was much in the way of distraction.

Apollo said something to his housekeeper and then turned to Sasha. 'Olympia will show you around, and take you to your room. I'll join you after I've made a couple of calls.'

Sasha took in the bright white spaces and minimalist furnishings as she followed the matronly woman through the villa. It oozed modernity and serenity. A contrast to the more traditional villa in Athens. Sasha liked it. She liked the starkness. The lack of fussiness. Its simplicity soothed some of her ragged edges.

Olympia led her down a long corridor and opened a door, standing back. She smiled. 'Your room, Kyria Vasilis.'

Sasha tried not to be self-conscious about the fact that she obviously had a separate room here too. She forced a polite smile, which promptly slid off her face as she walked into the vast room. Actually, it was a suite of rooms. They flowed into each other, no doors between them.

There was a vast bed with a four-poster frame and muslin drapes pulled back. The bathroom had two types of shower, one outdoor and one indoor, and a bath that was more like a private lap pool.

There was a dressing room and then a lounge, with its own soft comfy couch and media centre, with TV and a sound system. Perhaps, Sasha thought with an edge of hysteria, he was going to lock her in here, and keep her prisoner.

But then Olympia was signalling for her attention and Sasha followed her to the huge windows that were actually sliding doors leading outside to a private terrace, with sunbed and umbrella.

Olympia said in halting English, 'We will unpack your things while you take tea on the terrace. Follow me, please.'

Sasha smiled, silently trying to communicate her apologies for however she'd behaved before. Olympia led her back through the villa to the main living area again and out to a shaded terrace where a table was laid out with fruit and small cakes and pastries. Tea and coffee were in two pots, or there was sparkling water.

Everything was hushed and very exclusive. Sasha poured herself some tea and could feel herself loosening in spite of herself, as if she couldn't *not*, against this breath-taking backdrop. All she could see in the distance was the blue of the sparkling Aegean and the hazy outline of other islands on the horizon.

She didn't think she'd ever been anywhere so deeply peaceful. But apparently she had been here before, so why wasn't there even a tiny piece of recognition? Sasha fought off the feeling of frustration. She had to trust that her memory would come back to her sooner or later. It had to. And yet…with that assertion came a little shiver of foreboding.

Apollo stood in the shadows for a moment, watching Sasha where she sat on the terrace. She was wearing pale blue culottes and the white sleeveless shirt tied at the waist. She consistently seemed to choose the very opposite of what she would have gone for before.

He'd never imagined a woman in this place. There was something about the peace and tranquillity of this island that had always soothed a raw part of him and it had felt too personal to share, apart from with the islanders, of course.

He'd never brought a lover here, and he hadn't counted Sasha as a lover when he'd brought her here nearly three months ago. It had been a strategic decision.

But much as he hated to admit it, this time was very different from that first visit. She looked good here now. As if she belonged. In spite of that pale colouring. Her hair was down and it blew gently in the breeze, the rose-gold strands wavy and untamed. He could almost see her freckles from here. Freckles she'd always seemed obsessed with covering up, apart from that first couple of nights they'd met. He could still remember being fascinated by them on her naked body, the little clusters in secret spots. She'd been embarrassed…until he'd distracted her.

Heat gathered in his groin, making his muscles tight. Hard. He cursed. It was as if she'd had a personality change. He'd seen a film once about a man who had been ruthless and uncaring and who'd lost his memory in a shooting, and how, afterwards, his whole personality had changed.

Could it be something like that? Sasha looked troubled now, as if she was thinking the same thing as he was. He couldn't imagine what it must be like to know… nothing of yourself. A curious small ache formed in Apollo's chest. For a moment, he felt a sense of…pity? Concern?

She looked at him then, as if sensing him, and Apollo shoved down the fleeting moment of whatever it was. It wasn't welcome. He came out onto the terrace, shades hiding his eyes from the sun. And her.

'How do you like the villa?' he asked, sitting down.

Sasha sat up. 'It's beautiful, stunning. I feel like I've never seen anything like it, but apparently I have. And this island…it's so…'

Apollo took a sip of coffee, 'Boring?' he supplied.

She shook her head, looking away. 'No, not at all, it's so peaceful.' Apollo went still, looking at her suspiciously. Her voice was husky, as if she was genuinely moved.

She glanced at him then, her mouth taut. 'Don't tell me, I didn't like it the first time around?'

He shook his head, almost feeling slightly guilty now. 'No. You looked around and asked when we were leaving. You stayed one night.'

'Why did you bring me here the first time?'

Apollo's conscience pricked. He ignored it. 'I thought it would be somewhere you'd enjoy relaxing.'

'You mean, somewhere you could hide me away? Your inconvenient wife?'

Sasha stood up suddenly, shocked at how incensed

she was. 'What about now? Is this where you're plan-
ning on hiding me away until the divorce comes
through?'

She went to walk off the terrace, her sense of peace
shattered, but Apollo stood up and caught her hand.
Electricity sizzled up her arm, and she bit her lip against
the sensation.

'No.' And then, grudgingly, 'Maybe, the first time.
I wasn't really thinking. I was still in shock that you
were pregnant and how that was going to affect my life.'

Sasha looked at him, forgetting for a moment that she
hadn't been pregnant. 'What about my life?'

She flushed and pulled her hand free, walking a few
feet away. This was all so messed up.

Out of the corner of her eye she could see Apollo run
a hand through his hair. 'Look,' he said, 'we're here for
a few days. I've got some business to attend to with the
resort they're building and I've been invited to an opening of another resort on Santorini, not far from here,
later this week. You're still recuperating, so take this
time to rest and it might help your memory.'

Sasha looked at Apollo. She couldn't see his eyes
behind his shades. Just the hard line of his jaw. That
decadent mouth. The width of his shoulders and the
breadth of his chest. Her heart beat faster. 'You're not
leaving me here, then?'

Apollo's jaw clenched as if her words had affected
him. 'I'm not a gaoler, Sasha. When we leave here,
we'll sign divorce papers and we'll be able to move on
with our lives.'

'Move on with our lives.'

Whether her memory was back or not. Suddenly

the thought of going back into a world she couldn't remember was beyond intimidating. At that moment she'd never felt so alone.

Sasha looked vulnerable to Apollo, with a tiny frown between her eyes. Pale face. Very slight and slender. Yet he could remember the innate strength of her body as she'd taken him in so deeply he'd seen stars. The press of her breasts against his chest, nipples like bullets.

He took a deep breath, fought for control. He heard himself saying the words before he'd really articulated them to himself. 'I told you, Sasha, I'll make sure you're in a safe and secure environment. You won't be expected to navigate a world you don't remember if your memory hasn't yet returned.'

Something flashed in her eyes, an emotion Apollo couldn't decipher. 'Thank you. I appreciate that…after everything…'

She looked away from Apollo and gestured with a hand. 'This is paradise. Thank you for bringing me here.'

Her expression had turned indecipherable. Her voice and tone as if she were a guest. For a moment Apollo had to battle the urge to take her arms and force her to look at him, force her to reveal the emotion she'd just hidden from him.

Disgust at himself made him say something curt about checking work emails and he strode off the terrace, every cell in his body crying out for another taste of the woman who had torn his life asunder.

During the days following their arrival on Krisakis, Sasha found that with the peace and tranquillity she was finally feeling totally recuperated. And also it gave her mind time to settle too, and absorb all the revelations. The fake pregnancy, the divorce. Her behaviour.

Questions kept niggling at her—what had happened between them when she'd met Apollo and had then pretended to be pregnant? Why would she have done such a thing?

She still couldn't remember sleeping with Apollo. But she suspected she was remembering in her dreams, which were becoming more and more vivid and erotic. Last night she'd dreamt of him again.

They'd both been naked and he'd been kneeling between her legs, pushing them apart. She'd felt gauche, self-conscious, but all of that had dissolved in a pool of electric heat when he'd lowered his head and pressed kisses up the inside of one thigh.

She'd been shaking, trembling with need. Body dewed with a fine sheen of perspiration. And then he'd hooked her legs over his shoulders and he'd put his mouth to her *right there*, at the centre of her being. His tongue and mouth had done such things to her—she blushed in the late afternoon heat just thinking about how his tongue had felt, thrusting inside her.

She'd woken up, her nightshirt clinging to her damp body, heart racing, inner muscles clamping around a phantom erection. Mortified, she'd dived into the shower in a bid to bring herself back to reality.

She took a deep shuddering breath and forced her mind away from disturbing dreams. She didn't know what was worse—inhabiting her body in the dream or watching herself making love to Apollo from a distance. Both were equally disturbing.

She liked this time of the day best, late in the afternoon, when the intense heat of the sun had died down and it was more bearable. She'd found books on the well-stocked shelves of the informal living room and was reading a very unchallenging thriller. What did they call them? A cosy mystery? It was perfect for her exhausted and frayed brain.

She woke late most days, and wondered if she'd always had a habit of sleeping in. She was too scared to ask Apollo when he appeared every evening for their dinners on the terrace for fear of what he'd say.

He'd been gone every day from early, much like he had in Athens—presumably tending to business on the other side of the island.

They were both careful to stick to neutral topics at dinner, but Sasha couldn't ignore the growing pull she felt towards him. The throbbing undercurrent of electricity that sprang to life as soon as he came near her.

As if on cue, the small hairs stood up on the back of her neck and she heard a movement and looked around to see Apollo walking out to where she sat on a sun lounger near the pool, under an umbrella.

She was glad of the light covering of a kaftan over her swimsuit—the only one she seemed to own—as her body reacted to seeing him. And the memory of that dream. His clothes didn't help to calm her pulse. He was wearing board shorts and a polo shirt that showcased the bulging biceps of his arms and the hard pectorals of his chest. She saw dark hair curling just above the top open button.

As he came closer she said quickly, 'I'm wearing sunscreen. Factor fifty.'

Was that the slightest twitch at the corner of his mouth? He sat down on the lounger beside her and Olympia appeared with a tray holding two tall glasses of homemade iced lemonade.

He smiled at Olympia. *'Efharisto.'*

The woman smiled back, looking ridiculously pleased with herself. Sasha couldn't blame her.

Sasha watched as his Adam's apple moved up and down as he took a gulp of the drink. Even that movement was sexy. She took such a quick gulp of her own drink to calm her ragged nerves that she coughed and spluttered. Immediately he was beside her, a hand on her back. 'Are you okay?'

Eyes watering, Sasha could only gasp and try to breathe but all she was aware of was his hand on her back and the tight musculature of his dark naked thigh near hers.

When she could, she got out, 'I'm fine…fine.'

Thankfully he moved back to his lounger. He'd pushed his glasses up on his head and Sasha spotted something in his hair. Feeling shy, she pointed to his head. He ruffled his hair, dislodging fine dust. He grimaced. 'I need to take a shower, it's dust from the site.'

'Are you actually working on the site, too?'

'Just a little here and there. I like to be hands on.'

That only made Sasha think of how it had felt to have his hands on her thighs, pushing them apart, in the dream. Without even thinking about what she was saying, she asked, 'Could I come and see it?'

He lifted his brows in surprise. 'You want to see a construction site?'

She felt self-conscious now. 'If it's not too much trouble?'

His expression was bemused. 'Sure, if you want. I can take you with me over the next couple of days.'

Sasha smiled tentatively. 'I'd like to, as long as I won't be in your way.'

For a second something shimmered between them, a lightness. Then Apollo stood up. 'I'm going to go for a swim. Cool off.'

He downed the rest of his drink and put his glass down. Before he left he said, 'I'll see you at dinner? Unless you want to join me for a swim. I'm going to go down to the sea.'

The thought of swimming in the sea was immediately appealing but then something occurred to Sasha. 'I don't even know if I *can* swim.'

'Have you been in the water yet?

She shook her head. It had looked inviting but something had held her back. A wariness.

Apollo waited a beat and then he said, 'Okay, wait here, I'll be back in a minute.'

Sasha wasn't sure what he meant by that but it was apparent when he returned in a few minutes, carrying a towel and wearing nothing but short swim shorts. She stopped breathing. They were moulded to his hips and thighs. Their black colour only made his skin seem even darker. He was six feet plus of hard, honed male, not an ounce of spare flesh. He threw the towel down on the lounger and held out a hand.

Sasha averted her gaze from acres of honed olive-skinned flesh and looked at his hand suspiciously. 'What's going on?'

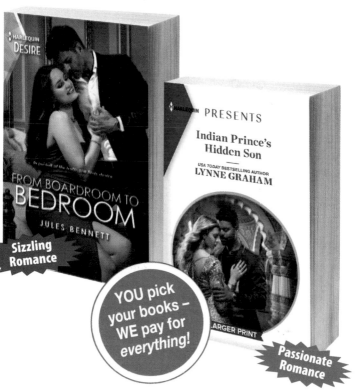

YOU pick your books –
WE pay for everything.
You get up to FOUR new books and TWO Mystery Gifts
absolutely FREE!
Total retail value: Over $20!

Dear Reader,

Your opinions are important to us. So if you'll participate in our fast and free "One Minute" Survey, **YOU** can pick up to four wonderful books that **WE** pay for!

As a leading publisher of women's fiction, we'd love to hear from you. That's why we promise to reward you for completing our survey.

IMPORTANT: Please complete the survey and return it. We'll send your Free Books and Free Mystery Gifts right away. **And we pay for shipping and handling too!** *We pay for EVERYTHING!*

Try **Harlequin® Desire** books featuring the worlds of the American elite with juicy plot twists, delicious sensuality and intriguing scandal.

Try **Harlequin Presents® Larger-Print** books featuring the glamourous lives of royals and billionaires in a world of exotic locations, where passion knows no bounds.

Or TRY BOTH!

Thank you again for participating in our "One Minute" Survey. It really takes just a minute (or less) to complete the survey… and your free books and gifts will be well worth it!

Sincerely,

Pam Powers

Pam Powers
for Reader Service

"One Minute" Survey

GET YOUR FREE BOOKS AND FREE GIFTS!

✓ Complete this Survey   ✓ Return this survey

▶ DETACH AND MAIL CARD TODAY! ▶

1 Do you try to find time to read every day?

☐ YES   ☐ NO

2 Do you prefer stories with happy endings?

☐ YES   ☐ NO

3 Do you enjoy having books delivered to your home?

☐ YES   ☐ NO

4 Do you find a Larger Print size easier on your eyes?

☐ YES   ☐ NO

YES! I have completed the above "One Minute" Survey. Please send me my Free Books and Free Mystery Gifts (worth over $20 retail). I understand that I am under no obligation to buy anything, as explained on the back of this card.

☐ I prefer Harlequin® Desire 225/326 HDL GNWS

☐ I prefer Harlequin Presents® Larger Print 176 /376 HDL GNWS

☐ I prefer BOTH 225/326 & 176/376 HDL GNW4

FIRST NAME

LAST NAME

ADDRESS

APT.#

CITY

STATE/PROV.

ZIP/POSTAL CODE

'We're going to see if you can swim.'

Suddenly reluctant, she said, 'I don't know if I want to know.'

'We'll go into the pool at the shallow end. You won't drown, I promise.'

Reluctantly, she stood up and lifted up the kaftan, very aware of the flesh-coloured swimsuit underneath. She avoided Apollo's eye, self-conscious and more nervous than she liked to admit.

He was still holding out his hand and after a moment's hesitation she took it, feeling his long fingers close around hers. His touch immediately soothed the nerves that had sprung from nowhere.

She followed him over to the steps that led down into the infinity pool. He tugged her along gently and she stepped in, the water a cold shock against her sun-heated skin.

He led her down until the water reached the tops of her thighs.

'Take my hands, keep coming.'

Sasha looked at Apollo. She took a breath and put her hands in his. He kept pulling her in until the water lapped up around her chest. She sucked in a breath.

'Now, come onto your front and just let me pull you along.'

Sasha shook her head, suddenly scared. 'I'll sink.'

'You won't. I'll be holding you. Your body is buoyant in the water. Trust me.'

Something about his voice was so…reassuring. So implacable. Sasha literally had no choice but to do as he said. She leant forward, putting her chest in the water, and suddenly her feet were off the bottom and she was floating and being pulled along, on the surface of the water, by Apollo.

When she realised she was no longer touching the bottom she panicked, her fingers tightening around his. 'Don't let me go.'

'I won't. Just keep looking at me and kick your legs.'

She kept her eyes on his, and did as he asked, tentatively kicking her legs. She could feel herself being propelled forward. Apollo leant back. 'Keep going, that's it.'

They went around and around the pool while Sasha got used to the sensation of being in the water, kicking her legs. It moved like silk along her body. No longer cold. Pleasantly warm.

After a while, Apollo stopped in the middle of the pool. He said, 'I'm going to let your hands go now. But I'll be right here. Just keep kicking your legs and use your hands and arms like this to move through the water.'

He mimed doing the doggy paddle.

Before she could protest, or say anything, Apollo was letting go and moving backwards, away from her. Sheer instinct kicked in and Sasha's arms moved of their own volition in a sloppy kind of movement, along with her legs. It was several seconds before she realised that she was following Apollo as he trod water on his back, moving away from her all the time.

She stopped and promptly started to sink once she'd stopped using her arms and legs. She couldn't touch the bottom here and her head went under the water. Immediately she felt strong hands under her arms, hauling her up before she could start panicking. She broke the surface, spluttering and coughing. 'You tricked me!'

He held her securely as her heart beat frantically. 'You were swimming, Sasha, and you didn't even notice.'

Her legs were scissoring back and forth as she took that in. Impulsively she said, 'Let me go again, I want to check something.'

'Are you sure?'

She nodded. He let her go and she moved her arms and legs frantically. Euphoria gripped her. 'I'm not sinking!' She had to be making the most graceless fool of herself but she was elated with this tiny success.

Then Apollo smiled. And suddenly Sasha's body stopped functioning and she slipped beneath the surface again.

When Apollo pulled her up this time she was choking with embarrassment, not water. The effect of his smile had almost drowned her. He was frowning now. 'Okay?'

She nodded, just then realising that his hands were under her arms, brushing the sides of her breasts. The corded muscles of his arms were like steel under her palms.

They were very close. So close that Sasha could see the darker flecks of green in Apollo's eyes. The start of fresh stubble on his jaw. Droplets of water clung to his skin. The dark curling hair lightly dusted his chest.

The air between them became charged. And she watched as his gaze seemed to fixate on her mouth and then drop, colour flaring across his cheeks. He muttered one word: *'Theos.'*

Sasha looked down too, and saw what he was looking at. The swimsuit had turned translucent in the water and she could see the pink buds of her nipples and the pebbled areolae as clearly as if she were naked.

Her entire body flooded with heat and she became all too aware of Apollo's naked flesh. All she'd have to do was bend her head forward and press her mouth to his chest. She wanted to taste his skin.

He muttered something else in Greek and started to tug Sasha back towards the steps. Her body felt like jelly. She wasn't sure if she could ever stand again. Apollo still had his hands under her arms and he moved her so that she was sitting on the steps leading down into the water.

He loomed over her, hands either side of her body. She was half in, half out of the water.

'What are you doing to me, witch? All I can think about is having you again.'

Sasha struggled to make her brain work but it wouldn't form coherent thoughts. All she could see was him and that sculpted mouth. She wanted it on hers. She was jealous of her body because *it* knew how it had felt to make love to him. But she didn't.

'Please, Apollo.'

'What is it, little flame? What do you want?'

Little flame.

It echoed in her head. He'd called her that before. He'd been lying beside her on a bed and her hair had been in his hand and he'd said, 'It's like a living flame...'

She forced her mouth to work. 'You... I want you.'

He brought a hand to her shoulder and with excruciating slowness pulled the strap of her swimsuit down. Anticipation prickled across her skin in goosebumps.

He dragged down the top of the swimsuit, baring her breast. He looked at it for a long moment before cupping it in his hand, a thumb rubbing her nipple, making her gasp.

And then he bent his head and his mouth surrounded her nipple in hot, wet heat. The same kind of heat she could feel between her legs. She tried to push them together to stem the tide, but Apollo was between them, his mouth on her breast and his hand moving down to cup her bottom, hitching her against him.

Apollo had gone past the point of restraint. Past the point of his last shred of control. He rolled the taut bud of Sasha's nipple in his mouth, feeling it swell and harden even more against his tongue. He nipped at her flesh gently with his teeth and then laved her with his tongue again.

Her body was quivering against him, like a taut bowstring. He dragged the rest of her swimsuit down and lavished attention on her other breast. When he pulled back both peaks were pink and wet. She was lying back, panting, her hair spreading in long skeins of red-gold in the water. She was like a sea nymph. *A siren.* Luring him to his downfall. But right now he didn't care about any of that.

He was throbbing with need—seeking a fulfilment he'd thought couldn't possibly be as earth-shattering as he remembered. But tasting her skin, feeling her shudder against him in response, he knew it hadn't been a one-off.

He looked down into unfocused blue eyes. Dark with

desire. Bee-stung lips. A distant sane part of his mind couldn't believe he was capitulating like this but he was only human and he couldn't resist…

'I want you, Sasha.'

Sasha looked up at Apollo. He eclipsed the sun and the sky. She'd never felt so attuned to someone else. The words he spoke resonated through her entire body.

'I want you too…'

His gaze dropped down over her body and he pulled her swimsuit up over her breasts, the wet material chafing against her sensitive breasts. She shivered slightly and he looked at her. 'Okay?'

She nodded, hands gripping his arms. 'Please… Apollo.' She wasn't even sure what she was asking for, just knew that she needed to be with this man in the most elemental way. Now.

He muttered something in Greek and gathered her into his arms, standing up from the water. But just as he was about to walk towards the villa he stopped.

Sasha was about to ask, *What is it?* when she heard the noise. The distinct *thwack-thwack* of a helicopter's blades. Apollo tensed. He cursed. Then Sasha saw it— the black spider shape of the machine, coming closer to the island.

Apollo walked over to the loungers, carrying her as easily as if she weighed no more than a bag of sugar. He put her down on her feet and she had to lock her knees to keep upright. He handed her the kaftan and said, 'Put this on.'

The sensual desperation that had been so urgent between them only moments ago now seemed like a mirage. Apollo looked grim. Sasha pulled on the kaftan, feeling the need to hide herself a little. Especially when she thought of how needy she'd just felt.

Still felt.

'What is it?'

Apollo looked at her and ran a hand through his hair. 'I forgot. The party in Santorini tonight. I arranged with the pilot to transport us to the party and back later.'

'Us?'

'Yes.' There was a burning intensity in his dark green gaze that made Sasha shiver all over again. He reached out and tipped up her chin with a finger, just as the whining roar of the helicopter's blades died down in the distance.

'You're coming with me. I know what you did and I can never forgive you for that, but, God help me, I want you, *agapi mou*. We will finish what we just started.'

Sasha jerked her chin free, his arrogant words setting something alight inside her. 'Maybe I don't want to finish what we started. Why would I allow someone who doesn't even like me to make love to me?'

She realised she was feeling hurt. And that was humiliating.

Apollo was shaking his head. 'This goes way beyond *like*. This is pure chemistry and I don't think either one of us is strong enough to resist it.'

Sasha felt conflicted. Torn between wanting to throw caution to the wind and acquiesce to his arrogant assertion that they would finish this, and wanting to pull back and defend herself against his mistrust.

There was a sound and Sasha tore her gaze from his to see Olympia appear. The woman said something in

Greek to Apollo. He answered and then said to Sasha, 'Go with Olympia, she will help you to get ready.'

After a moment when she felt ridiculously like a petulant teenager wanting to stamp her foot, Sasha followed the woman back into the villa. Who was she kidding? Apollo was right. There was a force of nature between them powerful enough to make her feel awed.

She felt an awful sense of futility because she knew that even in spite of Apollo's mistrust and all that had happened, if he so much as touched her again, she wouldn't have the strength or will to deny him. *Or herself.*

CHAPTER SEVEN

APOLLO WAS WAITING for Sasha outside the villa, by the golf buggy. She wasn't late but his skin prickled all over. He'd gone beyond the point of no return earlier, and there was no way now that he could, or would, deny himself where Sasha was concerned.

However inconvenient it was, he wanted her and he would have her until she was burnt out of his system once and for all.

He heard a noise behind him and turned around but nothing could have prepared him for the vision searing itself onto his retinas.

It was a deceptively simple dress. Off-white, sleeveless, it dipped in a V between her breasts, with narrow gold straps criss-crossing across her bodice, highlighting her high firm breasts and narrow torso.

It fell from her waist in soft billowing folds to the floor. Her hair was caught up in a bun, a plain gold band holding it back from her face.

She looked like a Greek goddess. Albeit with red hair, and pale skin and freckles. She made him think of the myth of Helen of Troy. Achilles, his brother, had used to love that story.

She indicated the dress. 'Kara packed it, is it okay?'

Apollo looked at her suspiciously. She was genuinely uncertain. Did she really have no idea how stunning she was?

'You look beautiful.'

Her face went pink. 'I… Thank you.'

Apollo desperately wanted to resist this act of innocence. It *had* to be an act. But his gut told him it wasn't. No one could keep up an act like this without slipping.

He couldn't stop imagining peeling that dress off her later, revealing her breasts to his gaze. Pulling up the layers of chiffon to find the centre of her body where she would be hot and— *Enough.*

The sooner he'd had his fill of her, the better. As soon as this crazy heat dissipated between them he'd move her into an apartment in Athens for the duration of the time it took for the divorce to be finalised. He would be done with her.

They reached the resort just as the sun was dropping in the sky. The was a palpable air of anticipation among the crowd assembled, the women tanned and lithe and beautiful, and the men in their suits.

She still hadn't fully regained her breath from the view as they'd descended over Santorini with its distinctive white and blue buildings perched precariously on cliffs over the caldera—an underwater crater—which had been formed in a volcanic eruption.

Not to mention the sheer magnificence of Apollo in a dark bespoke suit and white shirt. It was open at the neck, and he oozed casual masculine elegance and a raw sex appeal that reminded her of how needy she'd felt earlier, at the pool.

A hostess greeted them and handed them glasses of champagne. 'Welcome, you're just in time to view the stunning sunset. Please, make yourselves comfortable.'

The delicate layers of chiffon in her dress whispered around Sasha's legs. She'd never felt like a princess before, but she felt like one now. Kara had somehow unearthed this dress from all the more revealing ones in Sasha's wardrobe in Athens and for once she felt as if she was in something she might have chosen for herself.

Which was a weird thought to have…who else could have chosen her clothes?

Apollo took her elbow at that moment and led her over to where a terrace jutted out over the cliff edge, nothing but a stone wall between them and certain death. Sasha took a sip of champagne to try and alleviate the nerves jumping in her belly.

She pointed to a nearby town. 'That's Oia?

'Yes. That's where everyone goes to watch the sunset…give it a few minutes, you'll see why.'

They stood in companionable silence as more and more of the guests started to join them along the terrace wall. The sun was dipping lower now, casting out an orange and pink glow into the vast sky.

Sasha could see how the sun was bathing Oia in a warm golden glow, making the white buildings look even whiter. And then the sun touched the horizon and the world was bathed in pink and orange and apricot. It seemed to fill the entire sky and Sasha could see thousands of flashes coming from cameras and phones in Oia.

'It's stunning,' she breathed, deeply touched by the

natural phenomenon. And then just as quickly the sun was gone, leaving behind the faintest of pink trails and a bluish gloaming. Lights started to come on in Oia, like fairy lights in a string.

Reluctantly Sasha left the view behind to follow Apollo as they were led around the resort on a private tour. It was beautiful. Idyllic. A place for romance and decadence.

When they were seated at a series of long trestle tables, beautifully laid out with silverware and wildflower centrepieces, Apollo asked her, 'So, what do you think?'

Sasha swallowed a piece of delicious herb-infused fish. 'You want my opinion? But I don't know anything about this kind of thing.'

He shrugged. 'Still…indulge me.'

She took a drink of water and wiped her mouth with a napkin, hiding how pleased she was that Apollo cared for her opinion. 'I think this is beautiful, luxurious. I know I haven't seen your resort yet but I don't have to, to know that it'll be far quieter than here. Krisakis isn't overrun with tourists. How long would it take to get to there from here by boat?'

Apollo shrugged again. 'About two hours.'

'Krisakis could become a very exclusive day trip or couple of days' trip from here when it gets too frenetic. From what I've seen, you might not have the stunning geology of the caldera but you have peace and solitude and that counts for a lot.'

Apollo tipped his head to one side and regarded her. 'Not a bad assessment and you're right about Santorini being overrun.'

Again, Sasha was embarrassed by how Apollo's regard for her opinion made her feel. Was she so starved for praise?

When the dinner was over, the guests were led down to another level where a DJ was playing salsa music. The happy compelling beat resonated in Sasha's body. It was infectious.

Apollo pulled out a chair for her at a small table near where couples were already dancing, moving sinuously to the beat. He got her a glass of champagne. 'Excuse me for a second? There's someone I see that I need to speak to.'

Sasha feigned a nonchalance she wasn't feeling to be left on her own. 'Sure.'

She watched him walk away through the crowd, lithe and graceful, and saw how everyone he passed turn to look. Women especially. Her insides tightened low down when she thought of what he'd said. *'We will finish what we just started.'* He couldn't possibly want her that much. Could he?

A sense of insecurity assailed her. This party was peopled by some of the most stunning-looking women Sasha had ever seen. Women that Apollo couldn't fail to notice. What had happened earlier had been an anomaly. A heated moment.

She looked away from his departing figure and took a sip of her drink in a bid to try and pretend she was part of the wealthy crowd around her. The bubbles fizzed down her throat. That sensation, together with the uplifting music, the warm air, the scents, the vast starry sky, all conspired to make her forget her insecurity, and feel lighter than she'd done in days. Weeks.

Her toe tapped to the music.

'Come on! You look like you want to dance.'

Sasha looked up to see a young man holding out a hand. He was with another couple, and they were dancing energetically to the music. She immediately drew back, smiling, 'No, no, I'm just a spectator.'

'Don't be silly!' Before Sasha could object the man had taken her hand and was pulling her up from her seat. She spluttered a surprised laugh and put down her glass, with no choice but to give in to his exuberant invitation.

Apollo frowned as he looked over the heads of the people he was talking to. Sasha wasn't sitting at the table. Then a flash of billowing white caught his peripheral vision and his breath stopped in his throat.

Sasha was dancing—inexpertly, it had to be admitted—but all the more compelling for that because she was clearly enjoying her efforts, head back, laughing.

She was dancing with a young man who was swinging her round with more enthusiasm than skill. She stood out effortlessly and he could see people stop to look, smiling in spite of themselves at her sheer happiness.

A sense of possessiveness he'd never experienced before rose up before he could deny it.

He was jealous.

And then another emotion, less identifiable, made Apollo's chest go tight. He remembered she'd smiled like this when they'd first met. She'd captivated him like she was now captivating everyone here. And that's how she'd sneaked under his guard, by defusing a set of defences he hadn't even been aware of. A need to be controlled and on guard at all times for fear that the world would pull the rug out from under his feet at the next moment, like it had each time he'd lost a family member.

He'd believed his defences were impenetrable, vowing not to allow anyone to get too close, and certainly never entertaining thoughts of family—until she'd appeared and wreaked havoc.

You let her wreak havoc.

She'd exposed a weakness in him, a need for something he'd denied himself…and she was doing it again.

Yet even now, with this knowledge, he knew he wouldn't be able to resist her. A spurt of rebelliousness rose up from his gut. Why should he? She owed him…

Even before her dancing companion had noticed him and stopped and turned pale, Sasha was aware of Apollo's presence a nanosecond beforehand.

He snaked an arm around her waist and in the lull between one song and the next he said, '*Agapi mou*, the next dance is mine.'

Sasha might have laughed at how quickly her dance companion handed her back to Apollo, if her insides weren't coiling tight with awareness and something much sharper.

Apollo swung her expertly into his arms just as the music slowed to a more sultry beat. He was all around her and she could barely breathe because of her proximity to his tall, whipcord body.

To her relief, he didn't speak. Didn't say anything about the man she'd been dancing with, even though she hadn't missed the tightness of his jaw when he'd appeared to interrupt them. She didn't think it was for any other reason, though, than because here in public, no matter what had happened between them, she was his wife.

He pulled her close and after a moment of trying and failing to resist sinking against him, Sasha gave in, allowing her body to cleave to his. He held one hand up, and brought it in close between them. Her breasts were pressed against his chest. She stumbled for a moment when she felt the evidence of his arousal against her belly. She looked up and met that dark green gaze.

'You look surprised.'

Sasha swallowed, her previous sense of insecurity burning away in the face of this evidence. 'I thought... There are so many beautiful women here...' She stopped, feeling inarticulate.

'You thought I wouldn't want you?'

She couldn't speak or nod or move, and he stopped moving too so now people danced around them. He said, 'I won't stop wanting you till I have you again.'

He let her hand go and cupped her jaw and time was suspended as she waited for his mouth to touch hers. When it did she clutched at his jacket to stay standing. The kiss was all-consuming, and Sasha had no defence for it.

After long drugged moments Apollo broke the contact and pulled back. Sasha opened her eyes with effort, everything blurry for a moment. He was looking at her with a harsh expression on his face. 'What do you do to me?'

She had no answer because she could ask him the same question. A sense of urgency seemed to infuse the

air around them. Apollo took her by the hand to lead
her off the dance floor.

He stopped next to a couple of people and exchanged
a few words and then they were sitting into the back of
a car and being driven back to the helipad where the
helicopter was waiting.

The short journey back to Krisakis felt like a dream
and Sasha purposely kept her mind blank as if that could
help to not think about what was to happen, because
she was in no doubt where this evening would end. In
the reality of Apollo's arms and bed. Not a dream of a
hazy memory.

All was still and quiet at the villa when they returned. The air was heavy with the scent of night-
blooming flowers. Sasha took off her three-inch-heeled
sandals and relished the feel of the cool marble floor
under her aching feet.

Apollo took off his jacket and draped it over a chair.
He walked to the sliding door that led out to the back of
the villa. His back was to her and Sasha took a moment
to let her eyes linger on his tall, broad form.

He was so beautiful. Her heart gave a funny little
skip.

*Had she fallen for him after sleeping with him that
first time?*

Was that why she'd engineered a fake pregnancy?
Because she'd been so desperate to cling to him by
any means?

Was she in love with him now? Her heart thumped.
She knew he consumed her on every level. And she
wanted him with a fierce desire she didn't even really
understand. The thought of him casting her out of his

life made her feel breathless with pain. Not fear. So it
had nothing to do with the memory loss.

*Dear God, she loved him. Was that why she'd lied
to him?*

He wasn't moving but standing very still. For heart-
stopping seconds Sasha thought he might have changed
his mind. But then he turned around.

'Come here.'

It was a command. A command that Sasha could not
ignore or disobey, even if she'd wanted to. The relief
that he wanted her made her feel weak. She walked towards him and came to a stop in front of him. His eyes
were so dark they looked black. His jaw was already
darkening again with stubble.

'Take down your hair.'

Sasha complied, lifting her hands to where pins held
the bun in place. She took them out and her hair fell to
her shoulders. Apollo reached out and caught a strand.
'It's like golden fire…little flame.'

Sasha's nerves were tingling. Her breath came in
short choppy bursts. She closed one hand around the
pins and they dug into her palm. As if sensing she was
hurting herself, Apollo took her hand and opened it,
taking the pins and putting them on a nearby surface.

Then he caught her face in his two hands and moved
closer. All she could smell was him. The scents of the
island clung to him. Citrus, sea. And something infinitely more masculine and human.

She didn't need his hands to raise her face to his
as she was already doing it, every cell straining to get
closer, for his touch. When his mouth covered hers, she

wound her arms up and around his neck, telling him with her body that she wanted him.

Sasha could have happily stood there all night just kissing Apollo, but he drew back and took her by the hand, leading her through the softly lit villa to his room. Her dress whispered around her legs, heightening her sensitivity.

His room was at the opposite end of the villa from hers, with its own suite of rooms like hers, except much grander. She hadn't been shown this part of the villa and felt a little pang of hurt now to think of how divided they'd been.

But all her thoughts fled when they entered the room. It was palatial but minimalist enough to be a monk's cell. Albeit a billionaire monk. The sky was dark outside, cocooning them.

The massive bed was the focal point in the room. It didn't have four posters like Sasha's. It had no adornment apart from pillows and sheets. Stark. Like the expression on Apollo's face now as he turned to her. Sasha locked her knees in a bid to stop her legs trembling.

She'd never been more aware of the disparity in their sizes. Everywhere he was broad she was narrow, slender. He was tall, she was short. He was hard, she was soft.

His hands were on her shoulders. He tugged her gently but inexorably towards him. He tipped up her chin and bent his head, hovering mere centimetres from her mouth for a second. Then he said, 'Do you want this, Sasha?'

There was a tiny flicker of something in her brain at the way he said her name. Like something not fitting quite right. Like when she'd had that curious sense earlier that she hadn't actually chosen her own clothes. But it was too elusive to try and analyse or pin down.

Apollo was asking her permission to make love to her, when he didn't even have to. She'd answered him in the pool earlier that day. Her answer was in every cell of her body, in the rush of blood and liquid heat between her legs.

She nodded jerkily. 'Yes, I want this.' She put her hands on his chest, the heat of his skin nearly burning her hands through the thin material of his shirt.

His mouth touched hers and Sasha melted. One arm wrapped around her back and his other hand speared through her hair, cupping her head and holding it as he plundered and demolished any last coherent thought with his mouth and tongue.

He swept inside and explored with devastating precision. It was all Sasha could do to accept him and mimic his movements. He'd told her he wouldn't let her drown earlier in the pool, but she was drowning now, her arms and hands climbing around his neck, arching her body against his in a bid to get even closer.

This felt familiar.

New, but familiar.

She was barely aware of him undoing the zip at the back of the dress, and then peeling the straps of her dress down over her arms. The top of the dress fell down to her waist. He pulled back and looked at her and she could feel her nipples tighten under his gaze. The design of the dress had precluded her wearing a bra. She brought her arms up and crossed them over her chest, suddenly feeling embarrassed.

He stepped forward and pulled them apart. 'No, *agapi mou*, let me see you.'

There was a husky tone in his voice that made her feel less self-conscious. Feeling shy now, more than embarrassed, she said, 'I want to see you too.'

Apollo put down his hands and looked at her. Presenting himself. She reached for his buttons, undoing them one by one, little by little revealing that broad impressive chest with its smattering of dark curly hair.

When it was open he shrugged his shirt off and it fell to the floor. With efficient movements, he undid his belt, opened his trousers and pulled them down and off, taking his underwear with them.

He stood before her, naked. Sasha's eyes widened as she took in the sight of him. How could she have forgotten this? He was erect, long and thick. The head was glistening with moisture.

'If you keep looking at me like that, this will be over before we've even started.'

Sasha looked up, mortified. There was an echo of a memory now, feeling the same way, gauche. Inexperienced. Out of her depth. But before she could focus on it, Apollo was taking her by the hand again and leading her to the bed.

He sat down on the edge and pulled her in front of him. He slowly pulled the dress down over her hips, leaving her standing before him in just skimpy lace underwear.

He spanned her waist with his hands and tugged her forward, pressing kisses against her exposed skin, mouth and tongue finding a nipple and sucking it into his mouth. Sasha gasped and clutched his head, losing all sense of reason and sanity at that delicious tugging sensation.

Her legs finally gave way and he caught her, placing her back on the bed, coming over her on two hands. His eyes were glittering.

He claimed her mouth again in a kiss that felt almost desperate. It resonated inside Sasha and she matched him, stroke for stroke, reaching for him.

Apollo's hands were on her breasts, cupping them, thumbs stroking her sensitive nipples. Tension pulled tight low inside her. She felt empty, hollow. She needed him to obliterate those disturbing dreams. To replace them with reality. To finish what they'd started earlier, exactly as he'd promised.

Ever since she'd woken in the hospital with nothing but blankness in her brain, she'd felt rudderless. Here in Apollo's arms, his mouth fused with hers, she felt anchored again.

Safe.

He pulled back and Sasha realised how fast her heart was beating.

His mouth trailed across her jaw and down to her neck. She was panting. And her breaths got even faster when his hands expertly dispensed with her underwear.

His torso lay against her belly. Her thighs were spread wide to accommodate his body. His mouth lingered on her breast, teasing. She let out a little moan of distress and he looked up at her. 'Patience, little flame, patience...'

He dipped down lower, spreading her legs even further apart and he just looked at her there. A moment ago she'd been breathing like she'd run a marathon and now she couldn't breathe at all.

When Apollo put his mouth on the centre of her body she nearly wept.

She knew this. It hadn't been a dream.

Apollo was so drunk on the taste and feel of Sasha's body under his mouth, and his hands, that he almost forgot.

Almost.

At the last second, he reached for protection in his bedside drawer, ripping it open with all the finesse of a horny teenage boy and rolling it onto his penis.

He looked down for a moment after donning protection and almost came there and then. Her breasts were rising and falling with her breath, pink after his ministrations. Her entire body was flushed with arousal.

Her lips were swollen. Her eyes were huge and blue enough to make his breath catch, as if he'd never seen them before.

Making love with women had always been a short-lived thing—he'd gone through the motions dictated by society in order to find fleeting physical satisfaction— the chase, the seduction and the consummation. Invariably the seduction and the consummation never lived up to the promise. And Apollo had always chosen women who were experienced. The kind of women who understood not to ask for more. The kind of women who were not expecting anything beyond physical fulfilment.

But with Sasha there had been none of that. They'd met and combusted. There had been very little logical thought involved.

And right now all of his logical faculties were melting in a haze of lust. He notched his erection against the centre of her body, where she was so hot, and wet.

Ready for him.

He hadn't even entered her yet but his mind was already blasting back to that night in London and the way her body had clamped so tightly around his, sending him into orbit.

Something desperate caught in his gut. It couldn't possibly have been as amazing as that—and in a bid to try and prove to himself that he'd misremembered how amazing it had been before, Apollo thrust into Sasha's body, seating himself deep.

He saw her eyes widen even more, colour race across her cheeks. Her hands went to his arms, fingers curling around his biceps.

For a second he couldn't move, because in that moment he knew that the last time hadn't been as amazing as he remembered. It had been *more*. And that this was going to eclipse everything.

Sasha's hips moved tentatively and he nearly exploded. 'Please, Apollo…make love to me.'

A thousand horses couldn't have stopped him from obeying her entreaty. He pulled out slowly, feeling her tight muscles massage his length, and then…back in.

Sasha's body was moving with his in ways that were totally instinctive. She had no control. She was his. Body and soul. It was as if they'd been made to fit exactly.

Apollo came down over her body, twining his fingers with hers and lifting one hand over her head. His other arm was around her back, lifting her into him, deepening his thrusts even more.

A tight coil of need was building inside Sasha, a need for this tension to end, to explode. Apollo's rhythm was remorseless. He had the precision of a master magician or a torturer. Bringing her to the edge, keeping her there, stoking the fire but never letting it burn itself out...

Sasha cried out brokenly, her body dewed with sweat, her mind incoherent with need. 'Please... I...'

'Look at me, Sasha, look at me.'

Something inside Sasha went very still. She forced her eyes to focus on Apollo's face. That flicker was there again, but more than a flicker... Her name. It was *wrong*.

Apollo was saying, 'What do you need, little flame?' He moved and sent fresh tremors through her body.

Her thoughts scattered, flickers forgotten. She couldn't think, she could only feel. 'You...' she said brokenly. Apollo's powerful body moved over her, into her. Stealing her breath and her sanity.

She remembered this.

Being with him like this.

The next moment Apollo touched Sasha so deep and hard that she cried out as ecstasy tore her apart. Seconds later, Apollo convulsed with pleasure and his broken cry of 'Sasha...' echoed around the room.

She went very still deep inside, even as the powerful waves of ecstasy held her in their grip. Something cataclysmic had just happened. Shockwaves slowly obliterated the effects of the intense orgasm as the knowledge sank in.

At that moment of peak union, every cell in her body had rejected his calling her by another woman's name.

Because she wasn't Sasha at all. She was someone else entirely.

She remembered now.

She remembered everything.

Apollo was barely conscious when he felt Sasha wriggle out from underneath him, every touch of her body against his sending fresh flutters of need into his blood. Again. *Theos.*

He flipped onto his back just as he saw a sliver of pale curve of skin disappear into the bathroom and out of sight.

He was stupefied in the aftermath of one of the most erotic encounters of his life. The fact that the other most erotic encounter had been with the same woman made an uneasiness prickle over his skin.

But then his whole body went still when he heard the sounds of retching coming from the bathroom. He sprang out of bed and went to the doorway. The toilet was discreetly tucked away behind a wall and something held him back from intruding. 'Sasha? Are you okay?'

Nothing. Then a weak-sounding 'I'm okay, I'll be out in a minute.'

Apollo's mind raced. Had he been so consumed with his own insatiable need that he'd assumed Sasha had been with him all the way? He went cold—had he? But no. He could remember her nails digging into his hands as she'd begged him to keep going.

'Don't stop.'

He pulled a pair of sweats out of a drawer and put them on. He went back over to the bathroom door. Now he could hear the shower running—also hidden from view by a glazed glass wall. He paced back and forth for what seemed like ages, and then the water finally stopped.

He gave her a few minutes to get out, dry herself. He heard nothing. Impatience and something that felt like a tendril of fear made him say, 'Sasha? Are you sure you're—?'

But then suddenly she appeared, enveloped in a white towelling robe, and Apollo sucked in a breath. She looked like a ghost. Ashen.

Her hair hung in wet tendrils over her shoulders and the red looked dark against the white robe covering her body. He stepped back so she could come into the bedroom. She scooted past him, her eyes huge. Haunted.

Apollo's hands fell to his sides. 'What is going on, Sasha?'

She'd backed away into a corner, looking at him but not really seeing him. It was eerie. And then her gaze focused on him and her saw her throat move. She said in a broken-sounding voice, 'That's just it. I'm not Sasha.'

Apollo shook his head as if that might help him understand what she was saying. 'I'm sorry, what are you talking about?'

He noticed that she was trembling violently now. He cursed and went towards her, catching her hands. They were icy. Her teeth were chattering.

He drew her down to sit in a chair and knelt before her. Concern punched him in the gut. 'Should I get a doctor?'

She shook her head. 'N-no. I don't… I think it's just sh-shock. I can remember ev-everything. My memory. It's back.'

Apollo went very still. He'd actually forgotten for a moment. A cold finger traced down his spine. He'd become so used to *this* Sasha. He forced himself to focus. 'Are you in pain? Is your head hurting?'

She shook her head, more hair slipping over her shoulder. She looked very young. She looked scared.

He stood up. 'If I leave you for a minute, will you be okay?'

She nodded jerkily. 'I think so.'

She watched Apollo leave the room. She felt numb. She didn't even feel herself trembling but she could hear her teeth. She clamped her mouth shut and tried to wrap her head around what had just happened.

It had been the way Apollo had said, *'Sasha, look at me.'*

At that moment in her head, a very clear voice had said, *But I'm not Sasha.*

And then, when he'd said *Sasha* again, everything in her had rejected it, even as a powerful climax had torn her apart.

As if she'd known all along but had just blocked it out—she now knew everything. All the pieces of the puzzle were sliding back into horrific place.

She heard a noise and looked up to see Apollo return. He was holding a bottle and two glasses.

He said, 'Brandy.' He poured her a shot and handed her a glass. When her hand shook too much he put his hand around hers and lifted it to her mouth. She drank and winced as the fiery liquid burnt down her throat into her stomach. It worked almost instantly, sending out comforting tendrils. Creating a warmth between her and the numbness that had taken hold.

The shudders started to subside slowly.

Apollo poured himself some brandy and slugged it back. He held up the bottle. 'More?'

'A tiny bit.' She didn't want to become insensible, not when her mind was actually functioning again. She took another small sip and the warmth extended from her stomach out, creating a calming effect.

Apollo sat on the edge of the bed. After a minute he said, 'So, do you want to tell me what's come back exactly? How much of your memory?'

She forced herself to look at him. What they'd just shared... She knew that would be the last time he'd ever allow intimacy between them once she had finished telling him what she had to.

'All of it. Everything.'

'Why are you saying you're not Sasha?'

She took a deep breath. 'Because I'm not. I'm Sophy. Sophy Jones. Sasha is...*was*...my twin sister.'

CHAPTER EIGHT

SOPHY COULD SEE Apollo try to absorb this. Eventually he said, 'Twins.'

She nodded. She felt sick. Again.

He stood up. 'What the hell is this...some kind of joke? Now you're trying to convince me you're someone else? Did you ever have amnesia?'

Sophy stood up, even though her legs felt like jelly. 'The accident...happened. It was real. Sasha was driving, she'd picked me up from the airport.'

'Well, if you're a twin, and she was driving, where is she now?'

She was driving manically up a winding road, speaking so fast that Sophy couldn't understand half of what she was saying. And then she turned to Sophy.

'You have to seduce him, Soph,' she said. 'He wants you, not me. Isn't that ironic? He wouldn't sleep with me—he knows the baby doesn't exist now. But if you sleep with him you can get pregnant. Then there will be a baby.'

Sophy looked at her sister, her insides caught in a

vice of anxiety and confusion. 'Sash, what are you on about?'

And that was when Sasha took a bend too fast.

Sophy could see that they were too close to the un-protected edge and she called out. Sasha slammed on the brakes but it was too late.

They stopped right on the edge, the front of the car tipping over. Sophy felt nothing but blood-draining ter-ror as the ravine appeared below them, narrow, deep and dark.

She said, 'Sasha, don't move.'

She pushed through the gut-churning terror to open her door carefully and undid her seat belt. If she could inch out of the car then the weight would be redistributed...

Sasha was crying. 'Soph, I'm so sorry... I should never have done this to you. I've ruined everything.'

Sophy looked over and saw blood trickling down Sasha's forehead. She must have hit her head on the wheel.

She said, in as calm a voice as she could muster, 'Sash, don't think about that now. Just look at me, and keep looking at me—not down. I'll get you out.'

Sophy put her leg out of the car and felt for the ground. Then she eased her body so that she was perch-ing on the seat, her feet on the edge of the cliff.

She looked back at her sister. 'Keep looking at me, Sash.'

Sophy kept her eyes on Sasha while she reached out to try and get hold of something that might anchor her if she jumped free of the car.

But at that moment a strange expression crossed

her sister's face and Sasha said, 'I'm sorry, Soph, but I won't take you down with me.'

And then, before Sophy could stop her, Sasha was reaching across and pushing Sophy out of the car.

Sophy fell into space, her breath strangled in her throat, and then she landed on a hard surface, the breath knocked out of her body.

The only thing she heard before blackness consumed her was the faint sound of metal crashing far below her...

Sophy looked at Apollo.

Sasha was gone.

She tried to answer Apollo's question but her voice sounded very far away.

'She's in the car... I couldn't get her out. She's dead.'

And then, like when she'd landed on that ledge, far above the bottom of the ravine, darkness came over her again like a comforting cloak.

The next few hours passed in a blur. Sophy was aware of coming round and a concerned doctor asking her some questions. Olympia had helped her to dress and then they'd been flying over the sea with Apollo's voice in her ear.

'Are you okay? We're nearly there.'

When they reached the bright hospital in Athens where a team of doctors and nurses was waiting for them, Sophy knew that, as much as she wanted to, she couldn't hide from the painful reality waiting to be unearthed from the depths of her newly returned memory.

***

'It would appear that the trauma of the crash, of seeing the car disappear with her sister in it, along with the bump to her head, caused a classic case of trauma-induced amnesia. And, because her sister was in the accident, she blocked out everything about her sister, which was her whole life. Effectively.'

Apollo was silent. Taking this in. He was standing outside the private suite at the hospital with the same doctor who had treated Sasha—*Sophy*—after the accident.

Theos. Even now it was hard to get his head around it. No wonder he'd always thought of her as so pale. She'd been a different woman. He realised now that all those little anomalies he'd noticed since the accident hadn't been anomalies.

He didn't think he'd ever be able to excise the image from his mind of Sophy crumpling before him like a ragdoll and the terror he'd felt as he'd waited for the island doctor to arrive.

She'd come round at the villa but she'd retreated to some numb place Apollo couldn't reach. Even if the doctor hadn't recommended it, Apollo would have returned to Athens as soon as possible to seek further treatment.

Through the window he could see a detective talking to Sophy now. She was still deathly pale. Any lingering doubt he might have had about whether or not she'd been lying about the amnesia was well and truly gone.

It was too huge to absorb and try and figure how he felt about this, and the fact that Sasha—his wife, however inconvenient she'd been—was now dead.

The detective stood up and came out. He stopped in front of Apollo. 'I'll have a team sent to look for the crashed car immediately. And your wife's body. We should find Ms Jones's documents in the car if they haven't been destroyed. That will help clear things up.'

'Thank you.'

When the detective had disappeared the doctor said, 'We'll keep Sophy in for the rest of the night as a precaution, but she should be okay to go home tomorrow. It's going to take her some time to adjust to having her memory back. Be gentle with her.'

Apollo's mind was instantly filled with vivid images of making love to her with a desperation that hadn't exactly been gentle. His conscience smarted. Had sex precipitated her memory's return?

The doctor was waiting for his response. He said, 'Of course.'

She walked away and Apollo went into the suite.

Sophy knew when Apollo walked in. A volt of electricity went through her blood. Steeling herself, she turned her head to look at him. She quailed inwardly. His expression was stony. She had a sense of déjà vu from when she'd regained consciousness after the accident to find him with a similar expression.

'How are you feeling?' he asked.

'Okay, I think. My head feels full again.' She put a hand to it briefly.

Apollo looked at her for a long moment. 'Can you tell me one thing?'

She nodded, tensing inwardly. There was so much she had to explain but she needed to make sense of it herself first.

He asked. 'Was it you that night? The night we met?'

Something inside her relaxed a little. That was an easy question. 'Yes, it was me.'

An expression crossed his face fleetingly. Too quick for her to decipher. She tensed again. What would he make of that information?

He took a step back from the bed. 'I'll leave you now. The doctor said you need to rest. I'll come back in the morning.'

Sophy watched as he turned to leave. She only noticed now that he was wearing sweat pants and a long-sleeved top. Hair mussed. Not his usual pristine self. The thought that he hadn't showered since they'd made love made her skin prickle with awareness. She wondered how on earth she could be feeling so carnal after what had just happened.

After what she and her sister had put him through. He was almost at the door and on an impulse she called out, 'Wait… Apollo?'

He stopped and turned around. A muscle clenched in his jaw. 'Yes?'

Her fingers plucked at the sheet nervously. 'I just wanted to say… I'm so sorry. For everything.'

Apollo nodded tersely. 'We'll talk about it when you're ready. Get some rest.'

He walked out, closing the door behind him. That was the problem. Sophy didn't think she'd ever be ready to talk about it. She sagged back against the pillows. She felt more fatigued than she'd ever felt in her life.

There was little relief in remembering everything, even though she was grateful to have her memory back. To have *herself* back.

Sasha was dead.

She knew it instinctively, if not factually yet. There was no way she could have survived that crash. Sophy was still too numb with shock to fully absorb the death of her sister who she had loved more than life itself for so long. But who had also caused her more heartache than anyone else.

To say they'd had a complicated relationship was an understatement, but Sophy would never have guessed that Sasha would go as far as she had to engineer a good life for herself.

She'd also never forget that awful last haunting image of Sasha, pushing her free of the doomed car and saying, *'I won't take you with me.'*

For all of her faults and frailties, her sister had saved her twice in her life…

Oh, Sash…what did you do?

Tears filled Sophy's eyes and she turned her head to the wall, unable to stem the rising tide of emotion that engulfed her. She realised she wasn't just crying for her sister, she was also crying because she now remembered everything that had happened the night she'd slept with Apollo.

She remembered why he hadn't pursued her after their night together.

Because he hadn't wanted to see her again. Because she'd been inexperienced, a virgin.

And now she knew why. Because he'd told her he didn't *do* relationships after losing his entire family.

So not only had she lost her sister and realised she'd been betrayed by her too, she'd also remembered that she'd fallen for Apollo all those months ago, when they'd first met.

And they'd never had a chance.

Two days later

Sophy's nerves were wound tight. She'd had a reprieve of sorts from facing Apollo and the inevitable discussion since returning to the villa because he'd had an emergency meeting to attend in London.

He'd left her in the capable hands of Kara and Rhea and the doctor had come to check on her that morning. Apollo must have explained everything to his staff because at one point Sophy had attempted to start to tell Rhea but she'd just patted her hand and shaken her head, saying, 'You don't need to tell us. We knew something was different. We're sorry for your sister.'

Sophy had been inordinately touched, especially after everything Sasha had put them through. She knew how difficult her sister could be. She'd endured a lifetime of it and had never been quite able to break away completely.

They'd been living together in London and that was how Sophy had ended up covering for Sasha that night at the function where she'd met Apollo and where she'd had to call herself Sasha. It had been a classic Sasha request: *'Cover for me, Soph, please! This other thing has cropped up—I'll lose my job!'*

She'd done it, of course. Just as she'd said yes to most of Sasha's requests. After all, she'd owed Sasha so much... If it hadn't been for her sister, Sophy might not even be—

There was a sound behind Sophy on the terrace and she looked around. It was Kara. 'Kyrie Vasilis is in his study—he'd like to see you.'

Sophy's heart thudded against her breastbone. She'd known Apollo was due back but hadn't heard him return.

She'd dug through all of Sasha's clothes to find something vaguely suitable to face him and she'd found an unworn shirt dress, blue stripes, with a black belt. Wedge sandals. It was strange, looking at Sasha's choice of clothes now and realising why they'd never felt like *her*. Because she and her sister had always had diametrically opposed taste, in everything.

Sasha had been flamboyant, into fashion and pop culture. Always ambitious for a life more glamorous than the one they'd experienced growing up in a small market town outside London.

Sophy had been bookish and studious. Into clothes that made her fade into the background. She'd been happy to let Sasha shine but for the first time in her life she found herself wondering uneasily why it had been so easy for her to let Sasha claim the limelight.

She was outside Apollo's study now and had to collect herself. She knocked on the door and there was an abrupt, 'Come in.'

She took a deep breath and steeled herself but seeing Apollo after a couple of days' absence hit her straight in the chest like a sledgehammer. He was wearing a dark grey three-piece suit. And he'd never looked more gorgeous. His physicality was overwhelming, as if she was seeing him all over again with new eyes.

He was also a million miles away from the man who had been uncharacteristically dishevelled at the hospital.

Her heart skipped a beat and she sounded breathless when she said, 'Kara told me you wanted to see me.'

Had his gaze always been so dark green and unnervingly direct? He pulled at his tie and opened the top button of his shirt. 'How are you feeling?'

Dizzy.

But Sophy knew that had nothing to do with regaining her memory and everything to do with him.

'Fine. Much better. Thank you.'

He went over to the drinks cabinet and asked if she wanted anything. She shook her head. He poured himself a shot of golden spirits.

Something inside her ached. A few days ago she'd lain in this man's arms, their bodies entwined. Her soul had sung. Now there was a gaping chasm between them. And how could she blame him?

Apollo downed the shot he'd just poured. It did little to calm his thundering heart or douse the heat in his blood. He'd hoped that a couple of days' distance from Sophy and time to absorb all the revelations would somehow miraculously defuse this intense need he had for her…but as soon as she'd walked into the room his blood had boiled over.

He'd never expected to see her again after that night in his apartment in London. He'd told himself he didn't want to see her again but the relief he'd felt when she'd turned up in his office in London had made a mockery of that.

Dealing with Sasha had been easy because she hadn't been Sophy. Now he had to deal with Sophy.

He poured himself another shot and turned around.

Sophy hoped her emotions weren't as nakedly obvious as she feared. She'd never been as adept at hiding them as her sister. She had no idea what would happen now. What to expect. What she wanted.

You still want Apollo, whispered a voice.

She pushed it down.

Apollo came over and stood with the window at his back. It cast him into shadow slightly, making him look even bigger.

'I need to tell you something.'

She swallowed. 'Okay.'

'The detective contacted me. They found the car. And they found a body… They've identified your sister by her dental records and the DNA sample you provided.'

Sophy sat down on the chair behind her, the wind knocked out of her, even though this wasn't a surprise.

'Are you sure you don't want a drink?'

She shook her head. 'No, it's okay.' She looked at him. 'Did they find anything else?'

He nodded. 'Your bag, with your passport and personal items. There was luggage in the boot but it was ruined. Your things will be returned to you once they've been catalogued. They've ruled her death as accidental.'

Sophy sucked in a sharp breath. 'Was…was there any suggestion it wasn't?'

Apollo's face was expressionless. 'They have to look at everything. You'd just arrived on a flight from London that morning. Sasha picked you up from the airport?'

Sophy nodded.

'Yes.' Her voice sounded raw.

Apollo said, 'We can do this later, or tomorrow.'

She shook her head again. 'No, I know you have questions and you deserve answers.'

She steeled herself but wasn't prepared when Apollo said, 'I'm sorry for your loss, Sophy. I know what it's like to lose a sibling. I might not have liked Sasha very much but she was your sister and you must have loved her.'

Sophy couldn't stop the tears that sprang into her eyes. She stood up and fished a handkerchief out of the pocket of the dress. She went over to the other window and gathered herself.

Apollo said from behind her, 'We really don't have to do this now.'

Sophy swallowed down her emotion and turned around when she felt more composed. 'No. It's okay. Really.'

She said, 'I know Sasha was…a difficult person. More than anyone. But I did love her. I owed her a lot…'

Apollo frowned. 'What are you talking about?'

She looked at him. 'When I was eight, I contracted leukaemia. I needed a bone-marrow transplant. Because we were identical twins, Sasha's bone marrow matched mine so she was asked to donate her marrow.'

Apollo said nothing so she went on, 'She had no choice really, and she never forgave me for having to go through the painful donor procedure without the benefit of actually being sick and getting the attention. I think, unconsciously, I spent my life making it up to her.'

Sophy had never really analysed that before now but something clicked into place inside her as if finally she was acknowledging the role she'd given her sister out of a misplaced sense of guilt.

Apollo said, 'That must have been traumatic. The illness.'

Sophy made a face. 'A lot of it has faded with time. In a way, Sasha's constant demand for attention helped to distract from the memories…

'She was never content with what she had. She lied about our parents to people, friends in school. They were too boring for her. Our father was a postman and our mother was a part-time secretary for the local doctor's office. We had a perfectly happy home life, albeit modest. The worst thing that happened was that they both died within a year of each other, when we'd just left school. My father had a heart attack and then my mother contracted breast cancer.

'After they died, Sasha wanted to move up to London to make her mark. She'd never been happy in our little town. I went with her because the truth is I felt lost without her. She'd been the dominant one for so long.'

Sophy looked away from Apollo as she admitted that. She'd *let* Sasha dominate her, a dynamic they'd played out since they were children, exacerbated by her illness.

Apollo asked, 'Why is your name different from hers if you're sisters? Her name is Miller on her passport and papers.'

Sophy forced herself to look at him again. He was frowning. 'Sasha took our mother's maiden name, changed it legally—she thought it sounded more interesting than Jones. She did it when she was going through a phase of wanting to be an actress.'

Apollo paced away and back, and then stood at the

window for a moment with his back to Sophy. It all made sense in a sick kind of way. He'd met Sasha. He could attest to her ruthless deviousness. If anything, he suspected that Sophy hadn't really acknowledged half of what her sister had been capable of. The woman had tried to seduce him so she could try and get pregnant for real.

Her childhood illness... It tugged on him deep inside. Imagining a small girl with huge blue eyes and light red hair losing that hair because of chemotherapy. Being subjected to all manner of invasive procedures.

To counteract the sense of sympathy he felt, Apollo turned around again. Sophy's chin was tipped up, as if she was mentally preparing for the next onslaught. He pushed down the surge of something more than sympathy. He needed to know.

'That night in London. Why did you pretend to be your sister?'

Sophy's insides clenched with guilt. 'Because I wasn't meant to be there. I work—worked—as a receptionist in a solicitor's office. Sasha asked me to cover for her. She was double-jobbing at another event. It wasn't unheard of for me to cover for her like that. I didn't tell you my real name afterwards because I was afraid she'd get into trouble and lose her job with the event company.'

He frowned. 'Why didn't you tell me the following night when I took you for dinner? When we slept together?'

How could she explain how overwhelming it had been for a man like Apollo to show interest in her? Mousy Sophy. She lifted a hand and let it drop. 'I should have told you…but I couldn't believe that you wanted *me*. Sasha was the one who was confident. Glamorous. Not me.'

She shrugged minutely. 'Somehow it felt more appropriate to be her…not me.'

She winced inwardly, knowing how ridiculous that sounded. Apollo shook his head. 'I wanted you, not your sister. I think we've established that pretty comprehensively.'

A wave of heat, uncontrollable, moved up inside Sophy's body. She clamped down on her response, terrified he'd see the effect of his words. His gaze was too direct, too incisive. She felt as if she was being sliced open and all her vulnerabilities and frailties being laid bare for inspection.

She put her arms around herself and walked over to the window again, staring out unseeingly. Maybe if she didn't look at him as she tried to explain, it would be easier?

'The truth is that I felt out of my depth with you. Really out of my depth. You were suave and cultured. Way out of my league. Sasha was more experienced than me—'

Apollo cut in, 'You mean she wasn't a virgin? Unlike you.'

Sophy's face burned at that reminder. Her arms were so tight around herself now she was in danger of cutting off her air supply. 'I thought you wouldn't notice.'

'Well, I did.'

Yes, he had.

And Sophy could now remember his reaction in full glorious Technicolor. She remembered being so caught up in the moment that when he'd thrust into her and it had hurt, she'd tensed all over.

He'd looked down at her. 'Sasha? Are you—?'

Terrified he'd stop, she'd put her hands on his buttocks and said, 'Please, don't stop.'

For a torturous moment he hadn't moved. She'd felt impaled, stunned at the feeling of being so invaded, but then he'd started to move and the pressure and pain had eased.

What had followed had been nothing short of life-changing. Earth-shattering. She'd still been lying in a sated stupor when she'd felt him leave the bed and heard the shower come on in his bathroom.

A few minutes later, he'd emerged with a towel around his lean hips, his face rigid with anger.

'What the *hell*? You were a virgin.'

Sophy had reached for the sheet to cover herself, suddenly feeling very small and exposed. 'I thought you wouldn't notice.'

He'd emitted a curt, unamused laugh. 'Notice? How could I not? Why didn't you tell me?'

He'd spoken before she could formulate a response. 'I seduced you because I thought you were experienced... that you knew.'

'Knew what?'

He'd run a hand through his damp hair, muscles rippling, making Sophy's tender inner muscles clench again in reaction.

'Knew how these things go. Knew not to expect anything more.'

'More than what?' She'd known she'd sounded like a parrot but had been unable to stop herself.

'More than one night.' He'd folded his arms. 'I don't sleep with virgins, Sasha. If I'd known, I wouldn't have touched you.'

The thought that she might not have made love with this man had been a physical pain. 'But...why?'

A scarily blank expression had come over his face. He was like a statue. 'Because virgins are innocent and have expectations. The kind of expectations I can't, and don't want to, meet.'

'What do you mean?'

He'd emitted something that had sounded like a curse and his green eyes had narrowed on her face. 'Can you deny that you'd thought this was something more? That this wasn't just about sex?'

Mortified heat had flooded up her body and into her face. She *had* thought there was something between them. Romantic. Unique.

He'd seen it instantly. 'That's what I'm talking about. An expectation of something *more*. I don't do relationships, Sasha. I have no desire for a girlfriend. I have short-term relationships with women who know better than to attach emotion to the proceedings. This is just sex for me.'

She'd winced at that.

He'd said icily, 'This ends here now. Take a shower and get dressed. When you're ready I'll have my driver take you home.'

Sophy's focus came back to the present. It wasn't much comfort that she had more context now for why Apollo would have found seducing a virgin so unappealing. He was averse to relationships after losing his family. And she knew what that loss felt like. Ironic that they had so much in common.

She turned to face him, steeling herself not to show him how the memory of that night flayed her.

Apollo tried to resist the image of intense vulnerability Sophy displayed when she faced him again. Arms wrapped around herself. Her cheeks had two bright pink spots but the rest of her face was pale.

It didn't help that images of that first night they'd spent together kept intruding on his thoughts. The way her hair had spread out around her head like a halo of fire.

Little flame.

He gritted his jaw and bit out, 'We really don't have to continue this now if you're not up to it.'

She looked at him. 'No, I want to do this now. Maybe I will have a small drink, though.'

Apollo went over and poured her a measure of brandy. He brought it over and said gruffly, 'Sit down, before you fall down.'

She sat down again in the chair and he handed her the drink. He let her take a sip, and sat back on the edge of his desk. 'Were you and your sister in on the act together? Was she sent to me a month later because you didn't have the nerve?'

Sophy sat up straighter, a look of shock and horror crossing her face. 'That's... *No*, it wasn't like that. I had no idea.'

Apollo forced himself to resist trusting his first impression of her innocence. 'You weren't working together?'

'Not at all. How can you think that?'

'How did she end up in my office then? Telling me she was pregnant, if you weren't working together? How did she know if you hadn't told her?'

He saw the slim pale column of her throat work as she swallowed. She avoided his eye, as if ashamed. 'Sasha and I lived together. She knew something had happened...she eventually got me to confide in her. I told her your name. I know Sasha had her faults, but I never in a million years thought that she would use that private information. She looked you up, kept going on about how I should contact you, try to go out with you again...but I wouldn't.'

She looked at him again. 'After all, you'd left me in no doubt as to how you felt about seeing me again.'

His conscience smarted. Yes, he'd told her that but he also hadn't been able to get her out of his mind in the following days, weeks. Making a total mockery of his words to her.

Sophy continued, 'It was around the time of our birthday and Sasha said she was concerned about me, so she bought me a return flight to one of the Canary Islands for a holiday. I didn't want to go but she insisted.'

Apollo said. 'Go on.'

'By the time I got back she was gone. She'd left a note saying something about securing our future. Then I saw it in the papers. Your marriage.'

Apollo remembered the feeling of claustrophobia that day. 'If you weren't working together, when you heard about the marriage, why didn't you contact me to tell me who she was, who *you* were? That she was tricking me?'

Sophy looked sheepish. 'I didn't know about the

pregnancy. It wasn't inconceivable to me that you'd met Sasha and had been more attracted to her. That you'd wanted something *more* with her.'

Apollo felt a surge of anger mixed with frustration rise up inside him. Before he could say anything Sophy cut in, 'I know it sounds pathetic. But in a weird way it made sense. I'd been innocent and you hadn't wanted to see me again. Sasha was experienced…the experienced version of me. I felt like you'd seen something in her that I hadn't been able to give you, and that had made you fall for her. I know how convincing Sasha could be.'

Apollo grimaced at that. The fact that he'd fallen for her act negated his anger a little. Sasha had managed to dupe them both.

He stood up again, paced back and forth. 'Why did you come to Athens?'

Sophy fought not to squirm under that exacting gaze. 'Sasha rang me, she was hysterical. Incoherent. It must have been when you found out she wasn't pregnant. When you'd shown her the divorce papers. She begged me to come as soon as I could… I arrived the next morning.'

She went on. 'I couldn't even understand half of what she was saying when she picked me up at the airport. She was gabbling about you not wanting her, and that I needed to go and pretend to be her so I could seduce you…'

Apollo went very still. 'She was hoping that if you switched places, I'd suddenly want you and in spite of everything sleep with you and get you pregnant?'

Sophy avoided his eye. 'Something like that, I think.'

Apollo cursed. And then he said, 'The truth is that

she wasn't that far off the mark. As soon as I saw you again I wanted you.'

Sophy's face got hot again. She risked a glance at Apollo, who looked grim. He might be admitting he hadn't stopped wanting her but it didn't feel like a compliment. More an accusation.

'And if this crazy plan of hers had worked and you'd managed to seduce me and get pregnant, then what?'

Sophy felt sick. 'I don't know. I don't think she'd thought it through… I certainly had no idea what she'd planned. It sounded like gibberish to me.'

Apollo hated to admit that *if* Sophy had returned to the villa in Athens in the place of Sasha, and he'd wanted her as much as he wanted her now, she could very well have seduced him.

It was a bitter pill to swallow. He wanted her now. He was acutely aware of the buttons on the shirt-dress—how easily they would come undone, baring her to his eyes and touch.

No make-up. No adornment but her exceptional natural beauty. How could she have ever thought she was less attractive than her sister? The minute Sasha had turned up in his office in London he'd had an adverse reaction to her. Much to his relief.

At first you were disappointed.

He ignored that unwelcome reminder.

Sophy looked at him and he noticed the shadows under her eyes. He felt wrung out. He could only imagine how she felt.

'What happens now? I expect you want me to leave as soon as possible.'

Apollo couldn't stem the visceral rejection he had to

that suggestion. He told himself it was incredulity that she could think she could walk away so easily, not the pulsing ever-present desire in his blood.

He shook his head. 'I'm afraid that's not possible.'

Sophy hated the little jump in her pulse when he said that. He must despise her after everything. She wasn't even sure if he believed her. 'Why?'

'For one thing, we have a situation on our hands. Obviously we won't need to divorce now. But I've been seen out in public with a woman who is not my wife. A wife who has been deceased for some weeks.'

'We'll have to announce the accident and her death and the press attention will be intense. You'll be hounded when they find out she had a twin sister and that you were also in the car, but we can try to delay that until her death has been announced and the press moves on to the next story.'

Sophy frowned. 'How can you do that?'

'By taking you back to the island for a couple of weeks when the news is announced tomorrow. It'll keep you insulated from the press and it'll take about that long to process the repatriation of your sister's body. By then, the press should have moved on. Also, it'll give the authorities time to return your personal items.'

CHAPTER NINE

AND THEN WHAT? That was the question that had been
reverberating around Sophy's head for the past twenty-
four hours since they'd landed back on Krisakis. Olympia had shown her back into her bedroom, separate
from Apollo's. Sophy chastised herself. What had she
expected? For them to blithely continue where they'd
left off before her memory had returned?

Yes.

Her conscience stung. How could she be so selfish
when her sister was dead?

*Because it was your sister who was selfish in the first
place, betraying your trust, going behind your back to
try and seduce Apollo to further her own ends. Lying
to trap him.*

Sophy sighed deeply and hugged her knees tighter to
her body. Yes, she could blame Sasha for so much, but
also it had been *her* who had set this chain of events in
motion by not revealing her true self because it had been
easier to hide behind her sister, rather than believe that
someone like Apollo could possibly be interested in her.

The waves lapped up gently onto the shore near her
feet. It was soothing. It was also very quiet here on

the beach in the late afternoon. The heat was less intense now.

Since they'd arrived on the island, Apollo had been busy, either in his study in the villa or when he went to visit the construction site. They hadn't talked about anything since that last conversation.

Sophy knew she should be feeling some sort of cathartic weight lift off her shoulders, with her memory returned and full knowledge of what had happened, no matter how painful it was to face.

But she felt more tangled up than ever. Aware that her feelings for Apollo ran far deeper than she liked to admit. And she hated the sense that she was now a burden for him to deal with until the press attention died down.

Because surely he was just waiting for the earliest opportunity to let her go? Get on with his life? Say good riddance to her, and Sasha.

He couldn't want her any more. Surely his desire was well and truly eclipsed by disgust for what her sister, and she, however unwittingly, had done to him?

Sophy shut down her circling thoughts. Torturing herself like this was getting her nowhere. Apollo was keeping her here to protect himself as much as her from the adverse press attention.

The water was lapping at her feet now, refreshingly cool. She was about to move back but she was too slow as another wave on the incoming tide rushed in faster, soaking her bottom. She jumped up with a little squeal.

She was about to step back out of the way but another wave broke over her bare feet. Suddenly she was filled with a sense of longing to feel the water on her body. Even though the thought of walking into the sea terrified her. She remembered now why she couldn't swim and with a kind of sickening predictability it came back to Sasha.

They'd been very little and she and Sasha had been playing in a pool while on holiday. When their parents had been momentarily diverted, Sasha had taken the opportunity to dunk Sophy's head under the water, holding it there until Sophy had panicked and taken in a lungful of water, nearly drowning.

She'd been too terrified to swim after that, refusing to take lessons. Until Apollo had taken her into the pool that day.

Something defiant rose up inside Sophy. Anger and an impotent sense of rage at her sister—for all that she had done, for all that Sophy had allowed her to do, and for dying, before Sophy had got to tell her that she loved her one more time.

Tears were sliding down Sophy's cheeks before she could stop them, emotions overflowing. Obeying an urge she couldn't ignore, she stripped down to her underwear, pulling the sundress she was wearing over her head.

She wanted to feel a wave breaking over her head, as much to prove to herself that she wasn't scared as to cleanse something inside herself. Something she couldn't even really articulate.

At the last moment she looked around. The beach was entirely empty and private. Not another soul.

She could almost hear her sister's voice in her head. *'Go on, Soph, don't be such a scaredy-cat.'* It spurred her on.

She stripped off her knickers and bra and threw all her clothes to a safe distance from the incoming tide and took a step into the water.

It felt glorious—the cool water on her sun-warmed skin. She took another step and the waves crashed around her knees. Another step. She gasped as the water reached her hips and lower belly.

Another wave was approaching, bigger, and taking a deep breath, heart pounding, she ducked down, letting it break over her head. Instantly she sprang back up, sucking in deep breaths, skin tingling all over from the cold and exhilaration, and the decadence of being naked in the water.

Another wave was coming, and she ducked down for that one too, spluttering a little as she came back up, but suddenly she realised she was in deeper water that came almost up to her breasts and another wave was coming, breaking over her head. When she emerged again there was another wave almost immediately and suddenly she couldn't get her breath.

Before panic could set in, a strong pair of hands was under her arms, lifting her out of the oncoming wave. She blinked and spluttered, hands going out and landing on a wall of muscle.

'What do you think you're doing, you little fool? You don't know how to swim, you're not ready for the sea yet. You could drown out here.'

Apollo.

Waves were breaking around them now. Apollo's hair was slicked back from the sea. His face stark. He looked down and she saw his cheeks flush. 'You're naked.'

Sophy was gasping. 'I...didn't bring a swimsuit... I

wasn't going to get into the water…but I just…wanted to feel it against my skin.'

Her teeth started chattering, as much in reaction to Apollo as because the water was cold.

Apollo was grim. 'There's a storm coming, this tide is coming in fast.'

He swung her effortlessly into his arms and carried her out of the water. It was only then she realised how far in she'd wandered. Her arms were around Apollo's neck, her bare breasts pressing against his chest.

She burned with mortification but also something stronger.

When they reached the shallows she said, 'You can put me down, I'm okay now.'

He ignored her, long legs striding back up the beach. She could see a towel on the ground, near her discarded clothes. Apollo put her down and picked up the towel, wrapping it around her shoulders. He caught the ends and pulled her towards him.

She was very aware that he was naked too, apart from swimming shorts that hugged his body, leaving little to the imagination.

'What were you thinking? You could have drowned.'

Sophy blinked up at him. 'I wasn't thinking… I didn't expect it to get rough so quickly.'

She didn't even realise she was still trembling until Apollo cursed and started rubbing her skin with the towel. She wanted to say she wasn't cold—it was his effect on her. His eyes dropped and his hands stopped moving. She didn't have to follow his gaze to feel its effect on her breasts, nipples tight and sensitive after brushing against his chest.

She wanted him with a desperation she'd never experienced before. That recklessness that had sent her into the water rose up again and for a heady moment Sophy wondered if this was the real essence of herself that she'd repressed for so long, while she'd hidden in Sasha's shadow?

She dislodged his hands and the towel fell off her shoulders. There was something very elemental about being naked in front of him like this. Apollo's eyes flared bright green. His jaw clenched. 'What are you doing?'

Sophy also realised in that moment that she desperately needed Apollo to make love to *her*. To Sophy. To know who he was making love to this time. To call out *her* name. Exorcise Sasha from their past.

She opened her mouth but then she went cold inside. She'd just imagined seeing his reaction to her. He didn't want her any more. How could he after everything that had transpired? All her bravado leached away and she crossed her arms over her chest, looked for the towel. 'I'm sorry... I know you can't still want—' She spied the towel and bent down to retrieve it but when she straightened up Apollo took it out of her hands and pulled them apart, baring her to his gaze again.

'I can't still want *what*?'

'Me.'

'*Theos*. If only I didn't want you, my life would be infinitely simpler.'

He tugged her towards him and she stumbled slightly, landing against him, a sense of relief rising inside her. He took his hands off hers and cupped her face, tilting it up to his. Then he bent his head and covered her mouth with his in a kiss that was so explicit and carnal that Sophy lost all sense of time and place.

When he pulled back she felt dizzy, plastered against his body. She could feel the bulge of his arousal through the thin material of his shorts and put her hand down there, exploring tentatively.

He put his hand on hers. His voice was rough. 'Stop, unless you want to make love right here, right now.'

She must have communicated her desperation silently because Apollo muttered something unintelligible and let her go briefly to pull down his own shorts and spread the towel on the sand.

He pulled her down alongside him on the towel, shielding her from the rough sand with his body. His hands stroked along every curve of her body, sending her into a frenzy of need. Big hands cupped her buttocks, squeezing, kneading. Her hands moved over the wide muscled plane of his chest, mouth seeking and finding the blunt nub of his nipple, hearing his sucked-in breath when she explored with her tongue and teeth.

He put a hand in her hair, tugging her head back gently. Her vision was blurry.

'Sophy... I want you, now.'

Hearing her name on his lips made her feel absurdly emotional. She ducked her head into his neck. 'I want you too...'

He moved her over his body so that her legs were astride his hips. The centre of her body was embarrassingly hot and damp, but before she could dwell on that her entire being suffused with pleasure when she felt the head of Apollo's erection nudge against where she was so hot and needy.

He looked at her. 'Okay?'

She nodded. He notched the head inside her and she sucked in a breath. He put his hands on her hips. His expression was strained. 'Move up, and back.'

She bit her lip, every part of her being focused on doing as he asked. She came up and felt him under her, power barely leashed...and sank down, taking him inside her. It was the most exquisite agony she'd ever experienced as she felt herself stretch to accommodate his hard length.

She moved experimentally, up and down. Apollo's hands were on her hips, but not controlling her movements, letting her take the lead. It was heady.

A rhythm slowly built and built until Sophy couldn't control it any more. Apollo held her hips then, showing her how much restraint he'd exercised as he pumped powerfully up and into her body. She couldn't stay upright as she convulsed with pleasure, curving over him as he followed her over the edge and into an ocean of total and utter sated bliss.

As the after-shocks pulsed through their entwined limbs, neither one of them was aware of the incoming water lapping around their heated bodies.

Apollo hadn't intended to make love to Sophy. He'd intended to bring her to the island and put some distance between them. Giving himself time to assimilate everything. Absorb the reality that she was who she was. A different person. The same person.

And for about twenty-four hours it had worked out that way. He'd kept his distance—gone to the site, stayed in his study.

But then, this afternoon, he'd seen her far below on the beach. He'd seen her taking her clothes off, her pale body gleaming like a pearl against the azure sky and ocean, like some ethereal being. Not human.

Then she'd looked around, taken her underwear off. Stepped gingerly into the water. Then she'd waded further in, ducking under the waves. Apollo had felt like he was intruding on a very private moment and then he'd realised she was in danger of getting out of her depth. And that she couldn't swim.

When he'd reached her his insides had been in a knot and he'd hauled her up out of the water, her slim body far too light and puny against the might of the sea. He'd been angry.

Scared.

He'd also noticed that her eyes were red and he didn't think it was from the water. She'd been crying. Mourning.

He hadn't intended making love to her there and then. But she'd blasted through any resolve to resist her just by looking at him. Never mind being naked, her skin wet from the sea. Red hair in long silken skeins over her shoulders. Like a water nymph sent to tempt him. Or a mermaid.

The more he had of her the more he wanted. It made his skin prickle with a sense of panic. Exposure. The same kind of exposure he'd felt when he'd realised she had been a virgin, because he'd wanted her too much to look for the signs of innocence, and in hindsight they'd been there. He'd just ignored them.

Today had just proved her effect on him.

Dangerous.

He said, 'We didn't use protection today.'

Sophy's hand tightened on the stem of the wine glass. Heat suffused her body again to think of how carnal she'd been on the beach earlier. She barely remembered Apollo putting the dress over her head afterwards, dressing her. Leading her up the steps. Putting her to bed. She'd woken in her room, alone, as the sun had been setting outside.

She'd taken a shower and come out to find Apollo sitting in the dining area, clean-shaven, hair damp, as Olympia had laid the table for dinner. For a moment she'd almost been afraid she'd dreamt up the beach, but the storm he'd mentioned was lashing at the windows now.

They hadn't used protection. Because she'd all but begged him to make love to her.

She fought the rising tide of heat under her skin. Apollo looked at her and shook his head. 'It's amazing that you can still blush...'

That only made her blush even harder. 'It's okay... I'm at a safe place in my cycle.'

Apollo saw the worried look on Sophy's face. She couldn't hide her expressions. He had to acknowledge uncomfortably that he trusted her word.

'It won't happen again.'

Her face was still pink. Her hair was down around her shoulders. She'd appeared for dinner in long loose trousers and a loose silk top. It kept slipping off one shoulder.

The pink leached a little from her cheeks. She said, 'I think you're right, it's not a good idea.'

Apollo dragged his gaze up from where her pale

shoulder was bared. He frowned. 'What are you talking about?'

'Making lo—' She stopped. 'Sex. It's probably not a good idea. Considering everything…'

A visceral rejection of what she'd said rose up from somewhere deep and primal inside Apollo. He might have come here intending to keep his distance but after this afternoon that was an impossibility.

He shook his head and reached out a hand, finding Sophy's across the table and tugging her up out of her chair and over to him. He pulled her down and she landed on his lap, sliding into place like a missing jigsaw piece.

It's just desire, repeated Apollo like a mantra in his head.

He said, 'That's not what I meant.'

Sophy hated the way her heart leapt. 'What did you mean?'

'I meant that I won't be careless again, but we will be making love again. I don't see why we can't make the most of this. The chemistry between us is more powerful than anything I've ever experienced. It's unprecedented for me. But it will burn out. It always does.'

It will burn out. Sophy felt something inside her rebel at that assertion. This feeling that she'd never get enough of him…she couldn't imagine it ever fading away.

As if he could read her mind, he said carefully, 'Sophy, nothing has changed. I am not in the market for a relationship or family. It's not something I ever want to experience. If anything, believing that I might become a father has only confirmed my vow not to have a family. I had a family and I lost them, I won't put my-self through that again.'

Sophy's heart constricted. His words, painful as they were, actually helped to clarify how differently her very similar experience had shaped her. 'I lost my family too…but I know I won't feel whole again until I have a family of my own.'

Apollo tensed under her body and she held her breath. But then he said in a voice devoid of emotion, 'And I'm sure you'll have that one day. With someone else. What I'm offering is very transient. A couple of weeks to explore this insane chemistry before we part ways and get on with our separate lives. Once and for all.'

Sophy knew that she should stand up and step away. Tell Apollo that she wasn't interested in a transient af-fair. She wanted more. She'd always wanted more. It was why she'd still been a virgin long after her sister had lost her innocence.

But Apollo wanted her for now. Maybe that was enough. Maybe she would wake up one morning and not feel this insatiable need. Maybe she would be able to move on. Could she stand up and step back…from *this*? This energy pulsing between them even now?

She knew the answer. *No way.* Memories might be cold bedfellows in the future but she knew she didn't have the strength to walk away. Not yet. He'd been her only constant for the last few turbulent weeks. She needed to feel anchored again. Rooted. Even if it was only temporary.

She slid her arms around his neck. 'Okay, then.'

Apollo smiled and it was a smile of pure male satisfaction as he drew her head down to his and took her mouth in a searing kiss. A promise of what was to come, what he was offering, and she, like a miser, would take it.

CHAPTER TEN

A COUPLE OF days later, Sophy was lying face down in Apollo's bed. The morning sun was streaming in, warm on her bare back. A breeze chased the warmth across her skin.

Her whole body ached pleasurably. Since the other stormy evening, the days and nights had melded into one another, punctuated by moments of carnal pleasure— like last night. Apollo had returned from the site in the early evening. He'd taken Sophy down to the beach and given her another swimming lesson in the sea. They hadn't worn swimsuits, and they'd re-created the other day, except this time with protection.

Then Apollo had taken her back up to the villa and after a leisurely and very thorough shower, they'd eaten and gone to bed. But not to sleep. To discover new heights of pleasure and passion.

Sophy had been so crazed last night, so desperate for Apollo to release her from the sensual torture that she could remember her voice breaking as she'd begged him.

She buried her face in the pillow now and groaned softly, so she didn't hear when Apollo entered the room.

But she felt the bed dip and tensed. A tension that quickly dissolved when a finger trailed down her spine to the top of her buttocks.

She turned her head to meet a cool green gaze. *This* was what kept her from tumbling into fantasy land, this reserve that Apollo showed when he wasn't breaking her apart. The reserve that reminded her that he had rejected her after making love to her the first time. That reminded her that he'd only married Sasha out of a sense of duty and responsibility because he'd believed she was pregnant. That reminded her of his words to her that he didn't *do* relationships.

So, no matter what this was…it wasn't going anywhere. And she had to remember that.

'Kalimera.'

'Kalimera.'

She felt shy. Which was ridiculous. She turned and pulled the sheet up, covering her body. Apollo's mouth quirked as if mocking her attempt to be modest. She wanted to scowl at him.

'You mentioned before that you'd like to visit the site…would you still like to?'

That felt like an age ago now. She nodded. 'Yes, I'd like that.' Then she thought of something. 'Will it be okay for me to be seen here with you?'

'We won't be bothered here. It's entirely private. We'll leave in half an hour.'

Later that morning, Apollo looked to where Sophy was nodding studiously as his foreman showed her around the site. She was wearing those yellow capri pants and the white shirt that tied above her midriff. Wedge shoes.

A hard hat was perched on her head and a plait dissected her shoulder blades.

She could have passed for sixteen if it wasn't for the X-rated memories of how she'd taken him into her body last night, meeting him thrust for thrust, begging, pleading…sending them both over the edge and into a crashing, burning orgasm so intense— *Theos*.

She might have agreed to this transitory affair but he'd seen something in her eyes the other night that had caught at him deep inside. The same place that had been triggered when he'd believed he was to become a father, and when he'd realised that he wasn't as averse to the thought of a family as he'd believed himself to be.

In the aftermath of Sasha's lies, that weakness had been pushed down. Not allowed room to breathe again. Until he'd heard himself telling Sophy the other night that she would have a family one day. With someone else. Not him. He'd said the words and they'd felt like ash in his mouth.

He told himself it was sheer possessiveness of a lover. Nothing more. He didn't want more. Even with Sophy. Especially Sophy.

Apollo saw his foreman put a hand to Sophy's back to guide her over some uneven ground. That sense of possessiveness surged. He closed the distance between them in a couple of long strides, and took Sophy's hand. 'I'll take this from here, Milos, thank you.'

He was aware of Sophy looking up at him and his foreman's bemused expression. He ignored both and led her up to an open piece of ground at the top of a hill. She was panting slightly when they reached it. He let her hand go, and gestured around them. 'This is going to be the site for the solar panels. The resort will be entirely self-sufficient for energy.'

She was turning around, hand up to shield her eyes from the sun. She said, 'Does it have to be just for solar panels? This would be a beautiful spot for an exclusive suite. It would have three-hundred-and-sixty-degree views of the island and surrounding sea. Sunrise and sunset views.'

Apollo looked around and realised she was right. He followed her gaze, which took in the sea and hazy shapes of islands in the distance. The sky was so blue it hurt. Not a cloud in sight. All around them insects and birds chirruped and called. The scent of wild herbs infused the air.

He shook his head, his mouth quirking. 'I've had one of the best firms working on this for a couple of years now and no one came up with that idea.'

'Oh.' Sophy flushed, a dangerous warmth infusing her insides. 'Well, it might be a silly idea. I'm sure it was thought of and discarded for some reason.'

'We'll look at it.'

'Why did you decide to buy an island?' Sophy asked then, taking him off guard a little. Apollo looked out over the sea. 'When we were small, my brother was fascinated by the Greek myths and legends. My mother used to tell them to us at night as our bedtime stories.'

His mouth quirked. 'I found them boring. I was more interested in how things worked. He was the dreamer—he took after our mother. I took after our father. After our parents died and we were shuttled from foster home to foster home, he used to tell me that he couldn't wait to be old enough to leave Athens. Get on a boat and go to all the islands, see the places of the myths and legends. Athens was too harsh for him. He was too sensitive. He fell in with a gang, as much to survive as anything else. Once he started taking drugs…that was it. He was lost.'

Sophy's heart felt sore for Apollo and his brother. 'Why didn't you end up going the same way?'

Apollo shrugged, his eyes hidden behind dark shades. 'I guess I was born more cynical than Achilles. I was more street smart too. I stayed out of the gang's way. He was more susceptible. My father had always encouraged me to study hard, telling me that's how I'd make a life for myself. I put my head down and when I looked up, it was too late.'

The self-recrimination in his voice was palpable.

'You were kids. Your brother was older than you. It wasn't your responsibility to care for him. The adults around you should have been doing that.'

Apollo made a derisory sound. 'Our foster parents were just interested in the money they got from the state to take us in.'

Sophy looked away and out to the horizon again, a little embarrassed at the emotion she was feeling. The fact that he'd done this to honour his brother was beyond touching. The whole site for the resort had touched her—everything was going to be sustainable and designed to make the most of the island's natural resources, which in turn would help grow the local economy.

The resort was going to be seriously impressive and seriously luxurious. Private suites with their own pools, terraces and stunning views would be dotted around a central area where there would be several restaurants, a spa, a gym and shops, showcasing local produce and crafts.

In the main area there would be more rooms, and an infinity pool. Apollo also had plans for self-contained cottages where artists could come and stay in residence for a time—writers, painters, poets. They could apply for sponsorship through the resort and it only just impacted on Sophy now that he must have been thinking of his brother when he'd done that.

'Come,' he said, 'I'll take you to the town. I have a short meeting to attend with the town's council and you can get a coffee and look around.'

She noticed he didn't take her hand this time but she felt his fingers touch bare skin above the waistband of her trousers and it burned hotter than the sun.

Apollo was treated like a visiting celebrity when they reached the small harbour town a short while later. Old men came up to shake his hand, women smiled shyly, bouncing babies on their hips.

He seemed to be embarrassed by the attention, smiling tightly. He took Sophy's hand again, leading her to a shaded leafy square, with little *tavernas* that had seats and tables outside. She was glad of the shade as she was starting to wilt in the hot early afternoon sun.

He spoke to the owner, who answered him effusively, gesturing to Sophy to come and sit down. 'What did you say to him?' she asked, amused by the attention.

'Just to give you whatever you want until I come back. I won't be long.'

She watched him walk off. He was wearing faded jeans and a white polo shirt. The denim did little to hide the firm contours of his buttocks and when the owner came back with a menu, she was blushing.

He gestured towards where Apollo was disappearing around a corner and said something in Greek that Sophy couldn't understand, but she could see the emotion on the man's face and imagined that he was telling her how grateful they were that Apollo had single-handedly breathed life back into this little island. Just because he wanted to honour his brother's memory.

Sophy smiled and put a hand to her chest to indicate that she understood. The man smiled and said in heavily accented English, 'What would you like?'

She asked for a coffee, having developed a taste for the strong tart drink. She noticed that there was bunting up around the pretty square and women were decorating every visible area with flowers.

When they came over to the *taverna*, Sophy jumped up to help them string a garland of flowers over the front of the door. They spoke no English, she spoke no Greek but they laughed and smiled and for the first time in a long time, in spite of her grief, she felt light.

She was dying to know what the flowers were for but her attempts to ask the ladies made them laugh at her mimes. Then she saw them all go brick red and stop talking. They practically bowed down. Sophy had to stop herself from rolling her eyes at their reaction. She didn't have to look to know who was behind her. She could *feel* him.

She might roll her eyes at his effect on the locals but, really, she was no better. He came up alongside her. 'You're helping them prepare for the wedding?'

Sophy looked at him in surprise. 'It's a wedding?'

He nodded. 'The first wedding they've had on the island for a couple of years. It's a big deal…and we've been invited.'

'Oh…' Sophy's heartstrings tugged. She'd love to see a Greek wedding but she didn't expect Apollo would want to bring her with him, as if they were a couple. 'That's okay, they don't know about our…arrangement. You should go, it'll be expected.'

He looked at her and she felt herself flush. Was she being gauche?

'They invited both of us. It's no big deal. Greek weddings are pretty informal in places like this, everyone is invited.'

Now she did feel gauche. 'Oh… Okay, then. That would be nice.'

'I'll show you around.'

Sophy waved goodbye to the ladies and the *taverna* owner and when Apollo took her hand she tried to ignore the hitch in her heart. This was just a fleeting affair. No matter how much she might be falling in love with this lazy, idyllic island.

No matter how much she might be falling deeper in love with the man.

Her feet missed a step and she stumbled. Apollo put his arm around her to steady her. 'Okay?'

She forced a smile. 'Fine.'

Liar.

She couldn't ever afford to forget that she was only here because her sister had gone to this man and told a heinous lie, trapping him into a marriage. He never would have gone after Sophy. She never would have seen him again. She welcomed the dart of pain because this would be nothing compared to the pain she'd feel if she entertained fantasies.

The town comprised of a few artisan shops and a beautiful old Greek orthodox church that was being prepared for the wedding. There was a growing air of excitement.

Apollo led her down another side street and they passed a boutique. Sophy's feet stopped in their tracks. It was a simple boutique but there was a dress in the window that caught her attention. Caught her heart.

It was light blue broderie anglaise. Off the shoulder. The bodice was fitted and it fell in soft folds to below the knees. It was simple and unsophisticated. *Not* the kind of thing Sasha would have chosen in a million years. But she wasn't Sasha. She was Sophy and she wasn't sophisticated.

'You like that dress?'

Embarrassed, Sophy started to walk off. 'No, no, it just caught my eye.'

But Apollo didn't budge. 'It would suit you. Try it on.'

Sophy tried to desist but Apollo was tugging her towards the shop. The saleswoman had seen them too and was opening the door. Too late to turn back. She was obviously delighted that the saviour of the island was frequenting her humble establishment.

They went in and before Sophy could object, she was being whisked off to a changing area.

Apollo paced the floor of the shop. This was something he didn't usually indulge in—dressing his lovers. It would give the wrong impression. But right now he didn't really care. He just wanted to see Sophy in that dress.

He heard a noise behind him and turned. For a moment he felt like he couldn't breathe. He almost reached to his neck to loosen his tie but realised he wasn't wearing one.

He'd seen women in some of the skimpiest and most expensive haute couture but none of them had had this effect on him. The dress shouldn't be having this effect on him. But it wasn't the dress, it was the woman in the dress. She epitomised simple fresh-faced beauty. No adornment.

The bodice hugged her torso, around her high firm breasts and then fell in soft folds to below her knees. Her feet were bare. Her hair was pulled back, highlighting her slim shoulders and neck. He could see where the sun had turned her skin a light gold. She had more freckles.

His voice felt strangled when he said, 'We'll buy it.'

Sophy immediately started protesting but he just signalled to the owner that they'd take it and she whisked Sophy back to the changing area.

When Sophy emerged again Apollo was paying for the dress and accepting it in a bag. She felt conflicted—thrilled to have the dress but weird because he'd paid for it. Sasha had always favoured boyfriends with money who would buy her things and the sheer volume of clothes here and in Athens was testament to how much she'd squeezed out of Apollo.

When they walked out of the shop into the street Sophy said stiffly, 'I really didn't expect you to buy the dress.'

'It looks good on you, wear it this evening at the wedding festivities.'

He was putting his shades on again, oblivious to Sophy's turmoil. She didn't move. 'I want to pay you back for the dress.' She realised she had nothing, and not only that, she would have most certainly lost her job. There was only a meagre balance in her bank account back in England because she'd loaned Sasha money not long before she'd disappeared to Greece with Apollo. The knowledge that she'd most likely funded Sasha's trip to betray her made her feel even more prickly. 'I mean, when I can. I insist.'

Apollo looked at her. 'Fine. Whatever you want. I can get your people to liaise with my people and set up an electronic transfer for the princely sum of thirty euros.' His mouth quirked.

'Don't laugh at me.'

His mouth straightened. He put his hands on her hips and pulled her to him. 'I know you're not your sister, Sophy. You're nothing like her, believe me.'

'You couldn't tell us apart after the accident.'

Apollo arched a brow over his shades. 'Couldn't I? I never wanted her the way I want you.'

He kissed her there in the street, with people passing by. Sophy was aware of whispers and giggles and she couldn't stop her silly heart soaring.

When they returned to the town early that evening, Sophy felt self-conscious in the dress. She'd dressed it up a bit by pulling her hair into a bun on the top of her head and choosing a pair of Sasha's strappy silver sandals.

Apollo was wearing a dark suit and white shirt, open at the neck. He led her down to the smaller square where the church was located and the couple was just emerging from the entrance to loud cheers and clapping. Musicians played traditional Greek music.

Apollo and Sophy stood on the end of what looked like a receiving line of guests to either side of the couple, who passed down, accepting congratulations and good wishes. The bride was beautiful, with dark laughing eyes and long hair. Her husband was tall and handsome. They looked incandescently happy.

When they'd passed down the line, they walked through the town towards the bigger square. Apollo and Sophy followed them. The place had been transformed since earlier that day. Flowers festooned every available surface and fairy lights were strung across the square. Candles flickered on tables.

It was simple, rustic, humble and beautiful. Sophy knew Sasha would have hated it. She loved it.

Apollo was greeted and feted like a VIP. They were seated at a table for dinner near the bride and groom's table. A steady stream of people came up to converse with Apollo. Sophy was happy to let the occasion wash over her, enjoying the people-watching and lively Greek bonhomie and music.

When dinner had been cleared away, the music stopped suddenly and a line of men got up to dance, including the groom. Everyone turned to look at them. At the last minute they gestured to Apollo to get up and join them. He signalled *no*, but one of the men came over and pulled him up, amidst cheers and applause.

The music started slow and mesmeric, a familiar

Greek song, a traditional dance. Apollo was near the middle, near the groom. The men started dancing, slowly, in time to the music, arms around each other's shoulders.

Apollo did the slow deliberate steps with perfect precision, a smile on his face. He looked younger all of a sudden. Less intense. It made Sophy's heart swell, thinking of what he'd told her about his parents dancing. Maybe his father had taught him and his brother this dance?

The music got faster and the steps more intricate, Apollo's torso and hips twisting. He was so dynamic and handsome that Sophy didn't have to look around her to know that every gaze was trained on him. Probably even the bride's.

By the time the music built to a crescendo everyone was on their feet clapping and cheering. The men bowed. Then it was the women's turn, led out to dance by the bride.

One of the women grabbed Sophy's hand and pulled her up. She was shaking her head, laughing, but they ignored her. She caught Apollo's eye and shrugged helplessly.

Apollo watched Sophy being pulled away to dance. Her face was shining and she was laughing, trying to do her best to keep up with the steps of the dance. She stood out with her red-gold hair and blue eyes. Pale skin. She'd kicked off the high-heeled sandals and was in her bare feet.

Physical desire was like a tight knot inside Apollo, winding tighter and tighter. But along with the physical desire was something else, something far more disturbing. A sense of yearning…a need to replace the hollow ache in his chest. An ache he'd ignored for a long time. An ache he couldn't keep ignoring around *her*.

With her questions that struck at the heart of him: *Why did you buy an island?*

A sense of desperation gripped him now. This was just about *sex*. Nothing more. By the time Sophy had picked up her shoes and come off the dance floor Apollo was standing up to meet her.

He took her hand. 'Ready to go?'

She must have seen something of the urgency he was feeling because her eyes darkened and she nodded wordlessly.

Apollo paid his respects to the bride and groom and drove them back to his villa. All was quiet and hushed on this side of the island, only the faintest sounds of the revelry carrying on the light breeze. Sophy's feet were still bare.

They got out of the car and Apollo held out his hand for her. Sophy didn't hesitate. She took Apollo's hand and let him lead her into the villa, dropping her shoes on the way. The need to replace feelings he didn't welcome with the physical reminder of what was between them was overwhelming.

Sophy let Apollo lead her to his room. It was illuminated by moonlight. Standing in front of him, the lingering tipsiness from the wine made her bold. She moved forward and pushed Apollo's jacket off. It fell to the floor.

Then he undid his buttons and opened his shirt, pushing it off his broad shoulders. His chest was wide and powerful. She couldn't resist touching him, running her hands over his skin. His muscles tensed under her fingers and she felt powerful.

He reached for her hair and undid her bun, letting her hair fall down around her bare shoulders. She shivered at the sensation.

He caught her face in his hands and tilted it up to him. His features were stark with need and her insides clenched in reaction. There was something else there, some indefinable emotion. Instinctively Sophy touched his jaw with her hand. 'Apollo? Are you okay?'

Something expressive crossed his face for a second and then it was gone. Replaced by pure unadulterated *need*. 'I'm fine. I just want you. Now.'

She hesitated for a moment, because she sensed that there was some sort of internal battle being fought, but the clamour of her own blood drowned out the need to know. She turned around and pulled her hair over one shoulder, offering him her back. His hands came to the zip at the top of the dress and pulled it down, knuckles grazing the bare skin of her back.

The dress loosened from around her breasts and then fell to her waist. She pushed it off over her hips and it fell at her feet. Now she wore only her underwear.

Apollo came close behind her and she sucked in a breath when she realised that he was totally naked. His arms came around her, hands finding and closing over her breasts. Massaging them, teasing her tight nipples.

Instinctively she moved against him, and she heard an almost feral-sounding growl. Apollo turned her to face him and the electricity crackled between them. Urgency spiked.

He led her over to the bed and she lay down. He

reached for her underwear, pulling them down and off. He came over her, all rippling muscles and sleek olive-toned skin. She opened her legs to him, and he settled between them as if they'd done this dance down through lifetimes and not just in this one.

Sophy lifted her hips towards him, her small hand seeking to wrap around his rigid flesh, bringing his head close to where her body ached for him. For an infinitesimal moment he was poised there on the brink and then he took her hand away and joined their bodies with one powerful thrust.

She was so ready for him. She could feel her inner muscles clamping around him in a pre-orgasmic rush of sensation.

There was no time for slow lovemaking. It was fast and furious, both racing for the pinnacle and reaching it at the same incandescent moment, bodies entwined and locked together in an explosion of pleasure that went on and on. Sophy wasn't even aware of Apollo extricating himself from her embrace or of the way he stood up from the bed and looked at her for a long moment.

A week later, Apollo looked at Sophy across the dinner table that had been set on the terrace of the villa. She was talking to Olympia and the older woman's face was wreathed in smiles as she showed Sophy pictures on her phone of her newest grandchild.

Apollo marvelled at how he had been so blinkered by Sasha's deviousness that he hadn't noticed how different *this* woman was.

People responded to Sophy because she was open and kind. Polite. She was also sexy and utterly addictive. During the past week, Apollo had effectively shut out the world to gorge himself on this woman. But her appeal wasn't waning at all, or burning out. It was burning hotter. Becoming stronger.

He'd been ignoring calls from his office in Athens, to the point where his executive assistant had turned up on Krisakis today to speak to him personally. A visit that had broken him out of the haze of desire, shattering the illusion that he didn't have to engage with the outside world.

An image inserted itself into his mind—Sophy laughing and dancing with the other women at the wedding. The way seeing her like that had opened a great gaping chasm of yearning inside him. A yearning he'd had to eclipse by making love to her like a starving man. A yearning that lingered and caught at him under his skin. Chafing. Unwelcome.

A yearning that had made him careless. For a second time. Something he'd effectively blocked out all week. He was losing control, letting her in too deep.

Olympia was walking away with their plates now and Sophy looked at Apollo, her smile fading at the expression on his face. 'What is it?'

A stone weight made his chest feel tight. But he ignored it. 'We need to talk.'

CHAPTER ELEVEN

SOPHY FOLLOWED APOLLO into his study, her insides in a knot. He'd been distracted since his assistant had visited earlier. There was a spectacular view of the ocean and vast sky, which was currently a glorious pink and lavender colour. But that faded into insignificance behind the man dominating the space.

Apollo rested on the edge of his desk, hands by his hips. Hips that Sophy could remember holding only a few short hours before as he'd—

She blurted out a question to try and distract herself from memories of a week spent indulging in the pursuit of sensual oblivion. 'What is it, Apollo?'

But she already knew. It skated across her skin like a cold breeze. In fact, she'd been aware of it all week, even if she hadn't acknowledged it. The real world was waiting, just in the wings.

Even so, she wasn't prepared when he said tightly, 'When we made love…after the wedding, I didn't use protection that night. I told you I wouldn't be careless again but I was.'

Sophy's insides went into freefall. She hadn't even noticed, hadn't even thought about it afterwards.

Faintly she said, 'It wasn't just your fault. I should have been careful too.' It had been the last thing on her mind during that conflagration. Or during this week, when it had felt like their world had been reduced to this villa, this island. Apollo's bed.

You didn't want to think about anything that would burst the bubble.

No, she hadn't. She'd deliberately shied away from thinking about anything that might break the idyll. She'd let the fantasy become her reality. And now she would pay.

She almost put a hand on her belly but closed it into a fist. She said, 'It's okay. I'm at a safe place in my cycle. I'm sure of it.'

Apollo seemed to absorb that, and then he said, 'My assistant brought your personal things today, including your passport. And Sasha's body is ready for repatriation. My office will arrange everything for her funeral if you just give them the necessary information of where you want her buried.'

The cold breeze turned to ice in Sophy's belly. 'That won't be necessary, I can do all that.'

'I insist. She was my wife, after all. You won't have to worry about costs.'

Sophy swallowed. 'When do we leave?'

'Leander, my assistant, is still on the island, staying in the town. He will come for you in the morning and you will travel back to Athens with him, and then on to London with your sister. You'll be met by an assistant from my London office on the other side, they'll help you make further arrangements.'

Sophy searched for a hint of anything on Apollo's

face or in his eyes, but he'd retreated somewhere she couldn't reach. She'd noticed it when he'd arrived for dinner—when he'd avoided her eye. He'd been shut up in his office with his assistant for most of the afternoon.

'You won't be coming back to Athens?'

'Not just yet. I have some meetings here on the island to do with the construction and I'll travel back the following day.'

A sharp pain lanced her insides.

Her heart.

And also a sense of panic.

As if reading her every passing emotion, Apollo said, 'My assistant in London will make sure you're looked after, Sophy. You won't be left alone.'

If there was one thing Sophy wouldn't be able to bear, it was Apollo's pity or that she was a responsibility to be dealt with. 'That really won't be necessary. I can go back to the flat I shared with Sasha. I'll…be fine.'

Apollo stood up. 'Leander will be here before ten a.m.'

Sophy looked at him, in shock at the speed and efficiency with which he was apparently willing to dispatch her.

'So that's it, then?'

His face tightened. 'I think it's for the best. There's no point in prolonging something that we both know is at an end.'

Sophy felt emotion swelling inside her. If she'd known the last time she'd made love to Apollo was to be the last time, she would have imprinted every second onto her memory. 'You mean, something that never should have started.'

'Sophy…' he said warningly.

But a volatile mix of hurt, anger and fear made her say, 'The truth is that something happened between us that first night, we had a connection, and I think you used my virginity as an excuse to kick me out. To deny it.'

'You were inexperienced. Naive. I wasn't prepared to let you believe it would ever become something more than just sex.'

'Well, I think it was about you just as much as it might have been about me.'

'What's that supposed to mean?'

'I think you're an emotional coward, Apollo. I understand why it's hard for you to trust again. But I've lost my family too and I don't want to shut my emotions up for ever.'

A muscle pulsed in Apollo's jaw. 'Which is why I said to you that you'll go on to meet someone and have a family some day. You want more, Sophy. I don't.'

Sophy felt something inside her crack and break. 'I think you're a liar, Apollo. I think you do want more, but you're too scared to admit it.'

Or maybe he just doesn't want more with you.

Her insides curdled at that thought. Maybe Apollo would trust his heart again some day. When he met someone he couldn't walk away from, or shut out.

He opened his mouth but Sophy held up her hand, terrified to hear Apollo spell out that it just wasn't *her* who could crack the ice around his heart.

Now who's the coward? mocked a voice.

Sophy pushed it down.

'It's fine, Apollo.' She lowered her hand. 'It wasn't

as if you weren't clear about what this was. I'll be ready for Leander in the morning.'

Apollo watched Sophy turn to walk out of his study. At the last moment he blurted out her name. She turned around.

She said nothing. Her face was expressionless. Perversely, Apollo wanted to provoke a reaction.

'You'll let me know if there are any consequences?'

Her face leached of colour. 'You mean a baby?'

Now that he'd got the reaction he just felt hollow. He nodded.

Her mouth was tight. 'I told you, there won't be. I'm sure of it.'

She turned and this time left the room.

Apollo had nothing more to say.

To stop her from leaving.

He was so rigid with tension that he thought he might crack if he moved. *Theos.* Did he want there to be consequences? After everything that had happened?

Her words reverberated in his head, a mocking jeer.

'I think you're a liar, Apollo... I think you do want more...'

He turned around and stared blindly at the view. She was wrong. He didn't want more. He had decided a long time ago what kind of life he wanted and he wasn't about to let one woman change that.

One woman was no match for the demons that haunted him, reminding him of a loss and pain so great he thought he'd have preferred to die with them all.

All he felt for Sophy was physical lust. Nothing more. And that would fade. No matter how much it still burnt him up inside.

* * *

As Sophy's flight from Athens descended through stormy summer skies into London, she took in the unseasonably grey clouds. They mirrored her mood. Volatile.

She was angry with herself for having fallen for Apollo. For having revealed herself so much during that last exchange in his study.

The anger was good—it was insulating her from the sheer terror of stepping back out into a fast-paced world after living in a cocoon for these past few weeks. She knew that not far under the anger her shell was very brittle and fragile.

She had a sister to grieve and a life to re-start. A job to find because, as expected, when she'd rung them from Athens the day before, she'd found out that her position had been filled once she'd disappeared. The fact that they'd been so wholly unconcerned about her disappearance only compounded her sense of isolation now. Sophy shook her head, trying to dislodge that sense of isolation.

She put a hand on her flat belly. She'd not even noticed that they hadn't used protection that night a week ago. But Apollo had. She *was* sure there wouldn't be a baby and she hated herself for the hollow ache that thought precipitated.

Did she really want history to repeat itself, except this time with a real baby?

The plane had touched down. She lifted her hand from her belly. It was time to mourn and bury her sister and try to get on with her life and forget she'd ever met Apollo Vasilis.

Two weeks later, just outside London

'Let us go now in peace.'

Sophy stood by the grave for a moment. She was the only mourner at her sister's funeral. She'd told a few of Sasha's friends but they'd said they were too busy to come.

Sophy was sad, and a little angry—for her sister, in spite of her faults, had deserved better.

She had only barest sensation of prickling on the back of her neck before she heard the priest say, 'Welcome, sir. We've just finished the prayers.'

Sophy looked up and at first she thought she was hallucinating. Apollo looked taller and darker than she'd ever seen him. In a dark grey suit, white shirt and steel-grey tie. Dark shades hid his eyes.

Faintly, she said, 'Apollo…'

He dipped his head. 'Sophy.' He looked at the priest. 'Father.'

The priest came and took Sophy's arm. 'My dear, I'm so sorry. If you ever need to talk, you know where I am.'

Sophy tried to control her suddenly thundering heart. 'Thank you, Father.'

The priest walked away, leaving them alone by the grave. Sophy said, 'I wasn't expecting to see you here.'

Apollo's jaw tightened. 'I had always intended coming but I got delayed. She was my wife…however that came about.'

Sophy clamped down on the dangerous spurt of gratitude and something far more dangerous.

Hope.

'Thank you for your help in organising this.'

'It was nothing. I'll leave you for a moment.'

Apollo walked away and Sophy could see her own funeral limousine and then Apollo's blacked-out SUV. The drivers were talking. Apollo was standing at a respectable distance to give her some time. A gesture that made her feel surprisingly emotional.

She turned her back on him and said a few silent words to Sasha. The last few weeks she'd had to think about a lot of things and her relationship with her sister had been one of them. There was a certain sense of liberation now, but as much as that made Sophy feel guilty, she was also sad that it had had to come at the cost of her sister's life.

Her parents were buried in the same graveyard and Sophy walked the short distance to where they rested in their own plot, laying a flower on their grave.

Then she steeled herself to face Apollo. She turned around, aware of her sober black suit. It was actually the same skirt and shirt she'd been wearing the night she'd met him, and a black jacket. She'd put her hair up in a bun. She felt plain and unvarnished next to his effortless good looks when she walked towards him, where he stood under a tree.

She couldn't see his eyes but she could feel them on her and her skin prickled. She stopped a couple of feet away. He straightened up from the tree.

'Was the other grave your parents'?'

She nodded.

Then he said, 'Can we go somewhere to talk?'

The thought of being alone with him when she felt so raw made her blurt out, 'We can talk here.'

Apollo shuddered visibly. 'If it's okay with you, I've seen enough of graveyards to last me a lifetime.'

She felt a pang in her heart; so had she, come to think of it. She feigned nonchalance. 'Fine...where were you thinking?'

'My apartment in London, it's private.'

Where she'd gone with him the night they'd made love. A penthouse apartment at the top of a glittering exclusive building. The last place she should go with him, but suddenly the lure of seeing him again, however briefly, was too seductive.

'Okay.'

He stepped back and put out a hand for her to precede him to his car. He spoke with the other driver, who left. Sophy got into the SUV.

The journey into town was taken in silence, apart from a couple of phone calls Apollo made. Presumably to do with work. She wondered about Krisakis, how the resort was shaping up. A place she'd never see again.

They pulled up outside Apollo's apartment building and Sophy recognised it. It was bitter-sweet to have her memory back.

The driver opened her door and Sophy got out. Apollo was already standing on the pavement. Tall and gorgeous. Drawing appreciative glances from passers-by. Men and women.

Before, Sophy would have looked at Apollo and compared herself as someone who would fade into the background but she knew she had to stop taking on that role. The one she'd played with Sasha, allowing Sasha to be the noticeable one.

She was never going to set the world alight but she

could own her own space in a way she had never done before.

She walked ahead of Apollo into the building, through the door opened by the doorman. She could remember being here the first time, feeling so awed and excited. Tingling all over. Nervous. She felt as if she'd grown an age since that wide-eyed girl.

Virgin.

The lift took a few seconds and then they were stepping out into the grandeur that Sophy remembered. Lots of glass and plush carpets. Oriental rugs. Massive paintings on the walls. Sleek coffee tables with hardback tomes showing beautiful pictures of Greece and house interiors.

Of course, it had been dark outside the first time she'd been here and now it was bright daylight. And, in fairness, she'd only been interested in looking at one thing. Apollo.

He turned to her now. He'd already shrugged off his jacket and was loosening his tie. 'Can I get you tea, or coffee?'

Sophy held her bag in front of her. 'Just some water, please.'

He disappeared and came back a few minutes later holding a glass of water for her and a small cup of coffee for himself. He gestured around them. 'Please, make yourself comfortable.'

Sophy put down her bag and walked over to one of the windows, which took in the lush green gardens of Kensington Palace nearby. Truly this was a billionaire's address.

He said from behind her in a slightly gruff voice, 'You remind me of the night we met.'

Sophy fought to keep the blush down. She turned around. 'That's because I was wearing these same clothes. Pretty much.' The same clothes she'd put on with shaking hands and with tears blurring her vision after Apollo had summarily dismissed her. For being a virgin.

'How are you doing?'

Sophy's hand gripped the glass. 'I'm okay. I'm starting a new job as a receptionist in a central dentist's office in a couple of weeks.'

Apollo's blood thrummed with heat. A heat that hadn't cooled in Sophy's absence, much to his sense of frustration and a kind of futility.

'Apollo...what is it you want?'

He might have smiled at that loaded question, but it would be a bleak smile. He put the coffee cup down. 'I need to be sure...there are no consequences? After that night?'

His gaze dropped to her waist and he couldn't help but imagine it thickening and growing with his child. Before he could control it, that awfully familiar sense of yearning caught at his guts. *No.* Not what he was here for. Never that. Not even now.

Sophy blinked. He was so terrified of the thought of a baby that he'd come all the way here to check...again? She read his body language and something inside her curled up. *Yes.* He was that terrified.

She got out, 'No. I've had my period since I returned to London. I told you it would be okay.'

There was no discernible expression on Apollo's face

and Sophy was almost sorry now that she hadn't had another answer. To crack that facade.

'Okay...that's good, then.'

Except he sounded almost...disappointed. Sophy shook herself mentally. She was dreaming. She put down the glass in her hand and straightened up again. 'Was that it, Apollo? Because I really should be going now.'

She walked towards him and Apollo caught her hand as she was about to pass him. 'Wait.'

She stopped. She was so close she could smell his distinctive scent and she had to battle the memories threatening to overwhelm her. For a bleak moment she almost wished she could lose her memory again.

'Look at me, Sophy.'

Sophy really didn't want to look at Apollo. She was too full of volatile emotions. He'd only come to make sure she wasn't pregnant. But he wasn't letting her hand go. Reluctantly, Sophy looked up. Her pulse quickened in helpless answer to what she saw in his eyes. Desire.

He said, 'I still want you.'

A sense of desperation and anger that he still had an effect on her made her say, 'Well, I don't want you.'

She tried to pull her hand away but he held on tighter. He tugged her towards him, shaking his head. 'Don't lie, Sophy. Sasha was the liar, not you.'

'How do you know? You barely know me.'

'Don't I? I got to know you when you were your most genuine self. With no memory to inform you, you couldn't be anyone *but* yourself.'

She had never thought of it like that. She was so close their bodies were almost touching. Apollo finally let her hand go. She could have stepped back now but his scent was winding around her, keeping her there like invisible silken bindings.

He brought a hand to her jaw, cupping it. She wanted to turn her face into it, purr like a kitten. She could feel her will to resist Apollo draining away. She'd missed him.

So when he tipped her face up and lowered his head, she let him prove her words wrong. The kiss started out chaste, a touch to the lips, before coming back, firmer, more insistent. Encouraging her to open up to him. After a moment of hesitation she did, unable not to. Apollo swept inside and then she was lost, drowning in a whirlpool of memories and desires she'd tried to ignore and bury in the past month.

She could feel his hands roving over her back, cupping her buttocks. Just before she lost herself entirely, she pulled back, mouth throbbing. 'Apollo...what are we doing... It's over... You never wanted to see me again.'

'This isn't over.'

She pushed herself out of his arms, immediately feeling bereft. She shook her head. 'What are you saying?'

'Why does this have to end when we both still want each other?'

For a wild moment Sophy's heart soared. 'How would that work?'

He said, 'You could move in here, if you like. You said you're working in central London. I'll be in London regularly over the coming months as I've got a project starting up and I need to be on hand.'

Her heart dipped. 'You mean...this is just a temporary thing.'

'Well, for as long as we want each other.'

Her disappointment was so acute that Sophy nearly doubled over. Nothing had changed. He was just looking for an extension of their affair.

Sophy turned and walked back over to the window, not wanting Apollo to see the effect of his words on her. She spoke to the glass. 'So what you're talking about is essentially making me your mistress?'

Apollo looked at Sophy's slender back. He still had the taste of her on his tongue. The feel of her body under his hands.

'You can call it what you like, I'm talking about continuing this relationship.'

She turned around. 'But just the physical side of it. And once that's fizzled out then we get on with our lives?'

Frustration bit into Apollo. 'Can you walk away from what's between us?'

She came closer and to his shock he saw moisture in her eyes. It was like a punch to the gut.

She said, 'No, I can't walk away. But I'll have to. You see, I want more than that, Apollo. Much more. And, unlike you, I'm not prepared to settle for less.'

Panic gripped Apollo. He felt like he was slipping down a cliff-edge with nothing to hold onto. He said, 'How much do you want?'

She looked at him, an expression of shock and then disgust crossing her face. 'No. I'm not talking about money. I'm talking about *love*. Family. Emotions. All the things you don't want.'

As if money could buy a woman like Sophy. He felt ashamed. A great yawning chasm was opening inside

Apollo—the place where he'd almost lost himself after Achilles had died. When he'd felt so terrified and alone. Abandoned. Sophy was looking at him with those huge eyes, asking him to step into that place.

He shook his head, stepped back. 'I've told you, I can't give you that.'

Sophy felt her heart crack. 'Can't...or won't?'

She wasn't expecting an answer, so she stepped around Apollo and walked towards the corridor leading to the elevator to take her back down to reality.

But she couldn't go without telling him... She turned back and he was looking after her, jaw tight.

She said, 'I love you, Apollo. I fell for you the night we met. I'm so sorry for what my sister put you through, but I'm glad that her actions brought us together because I might never have seen you again.'

She turned and walked out, hoping stupidly that she'd hear her voice or feel his hand on her arm. But there was nothing. She got into the elevator and the doors closed. It descended. She got out and walked forward and out of the building like an automaton.

She went down into the nearest tube station and followed the crowd through the turnstile, not even sure where she was going. She was numb. But she welcomed the numbness, which was protecting her from incredible pain.

You could have stayed...become his mistress.

She shut the voice out. It would have killed her in the end.

She walked towards the signs for the Bakerloo Line, which would take her back to south London. At the top of the escalator, though, she heard a call.

'Sophy!'

No. It was her stupid mind playing tricks. She was about to step onto the escalator and it came again, urgent.

'Sophy, wait. Please!'

She heard a girl near her say, '*I'll* be Sophy if he wants. He's *gorgeous*.'

Sophy turned around. Apollo was standing on the other side of the turnstiles with his hands braced on the sides—as if ready to vault over. Sophy walked towards him, trying not to let a flame of hope spring to life.

He looked wild. She could feel the electric pull between them, even here.

She came closer. 'I won't be your mistress, Apollo. I'm not mistress material.'

He said, 'I don't want you to be my mistress, Sophy... just come back over here, please?'

Sophy was aware of a crowd gathering. People whispering. Slowly, she walked over to the exit turnstiles and came back through. Apollo had tracked her progress from the other side, his eyes never leaving hers. He was waiting for her. Big, solid.

Sophy knew if he asked her again she wouldn't have the strength to say no. She knew she was weak enough to clutch at any more time he would give her to be with him.

She stopped in front of him and he put his hands on her arms. 'I'm sorry,' he said.

'For what?'

'For disrespecting you. And for the ten seconds too long that it took me to remove my head from my—'

A public announcement blared at that moment,

blocking out Apollo's words, but Sophy could guess what he'd said.

She was too full of trepidation to let the bubble of euphoria she felt rise up inside her. 'What are you saying, Apollo?'

'I'm saying that it's too late. Any hope I might have had of protecting myself against the pain of losing you—letting you go in Athens, trying to make you my temporary lover—is well and truly shattered. Because I would prefer to spend one more perfect day with you, if that's all we have, than a lifetime of regret because I was too much of a coward to admit my fears and open my heart.'

Sophy heard someone sigh near them, but Apollo filled her vision. And her rapidly swelling heart. 'Are you saying...?'

'That I love you. Deeply, irrevocably. Infinitely. I fell for you the moment you looked at me for the first time but I didn't know it at the time. All I knew was that I had to have you.'

He tugged her towards him. 'Please...don't walk away from me. Give me a chance.'

Sophy shook her head. Suddenly she was the one who was scared. She whispered, 'I can't do this, Apollo. It'll kill me if you're just saying this to get me back in your bed.'

He kissed her then. In the middle of the concourse of one of London's busiest Tube stations. A deep kiss, full of remorse and pain and...love. A promise.

They broke apart and Apollo looked at her. They were oblivious to the crowd that had formed around them, phones raised.

'All I can do is ask you to trust me. I *do* want more. You've made me want more, and I've denied it to myself, or tried to, but I can't any longer. I want you, Sophy, and I want to spend the rest of my life with you. Will you give me a chance to prove that to you?'

A voice nearby said loudly, 'If you won't, love, I will!'

A giggle of pure emotion burst up from Sophy's belly. Along with hope…a hope that she couldn't push back down. She smiled a wobbly smile. 'One chance.'

His eyes burned like dark emeralds. He took her hand and raised it to his lips. 'One chance is all I need.' He took her hand and led her back up, out of the dark underground and into the light. The sunlight made everything shimmer. It felt like a benediction. A new start. And Sophy took a deep breath and let herself trust.

Sophy looked out over the sight of the city waking up to a brand-new day under a pink dawn. She was wrapped in a voluminous robe and her body felt pleasantly lethargic and sated. She'd left a sleeping Apollo on the bed, his brow smooth in sleep.

She was still trying to absorb what had happened and she couldn't help but feel slightly fearful that it had all been a dream. Or had she projected her love onto Apollo so much that she'd heard what she'd wanted to—and he hadn't actually made those declarations…

'Here you are.'

She tensed against his inevitable effect on her, but it was useless when his arms slid around her waist and he brought his body flush with hers. He said into her ear,

'When I woke up just now, and I was alone in the bed, I thought I'd dreamed it all up. That you were gone.'

Sophy turned around in Apollo's arms and looked up at him. 'I was just afraid of the same thing, that I'd imagined it all…that you hadn't said—'

'That I love you?'

She nodded her head, biting her lip.

'Well, I did. And I do. I love you, Sophy Jones. And if it's all right with you, I'd like us to marry as soon as possible.'

Her heart skipped a beat. 'Was that a proposal?'

He looked worried. 'I can make it more romantic if you like…'

She shook her head and smiled. 'No, that'll do just fine. And, yes, I accept your proposal.'

But then she sobered again. Apollo tipped her chin up. 'What is it?'

She put her hands on his bare chest. He'd pulled on sweats but she had to not let his physicality distract her.

'What I said about a family… I meant that. I do want a family. Children. When you reminded me that we hadn't used protection…for a moment, even though it would have been the wrong thing, I wanted there to be a baby.'

He cupped her face. 'I told myself I didn't want there to be a baby and that's why I was so concerned about *consequences*, but actually I think deep down I was hoping that you might have got pregnant. I had to come to terms with the thought of a baby when I thought Sasha was pregnant and what surprised me was how much I wanted it. In spite of everything I'd been telling

myself for years. Except, in that situation, I compart-
mentalised the baby very separately from its mother.'

'But now…with you… I want it all too. The baby,
you. Us, together. Making a life. It scared me for so
long, the thought of losing someone I love, so I blocked
it out. That's why I was so harsh with you after we slept
together that first night. I knew you'd got to me more
than any other woman ever had. So I used your virginity as an excuse to get you to leave. But I never forgot
about you…and I think eventually the memory of you
would have driven me so mad that I would have come
to find you.

'But then your sister turned up…and I was relieved
I hadn't had to be the one to make a move. Until I realised I no longer wanted you. And then Sasha dropped
her bombshell. I told myself I was glad I didn't desire
you, because then it meant what we'd shared couldn't
have been as amazing as I remembered…but then that
all got blown out of the water…'

Sophy looked at him, finally believing and trusting.
But he said, 'Need more convincing?'

She nodded and started moving her hands down to
his waist. His body hardened against hers. 'Maybe a
little more…just to make sure we're on the same page.'

Apollo scooped her up and carried her back into the
bedroom and put her down on her feet by the bed. He
undid the belt of the robe and tugged it off her body. His
green gaze glittered with barely banked heat as it swept
up and down her body. He muttered, 'I will never get
tired of looking at you, little flame. Or wanting you.'

He kissed her then and she arched into him, pouring
all of her love into the kiss. His sweats got discarded

and they landed on the bed in a tangle of limbs. When Apollo was poised to enter her, Sophy put her hands on his hips. He wasn't wearing protection. She said huskily, 'Are you sure…it's not too soon?'

He bent down and pressed his lips to hers and then he said, 'It's not soon enough, *agapi mou*.'

And Sophy knew, as Apollo joined his body to hers, that he meant every word, and that today was the start of a new life. For them and for ever.

EPILOGUE

Three and a half years later, Krisakis

'MAMA, LOOK! I'M SWIMMING!'

Sophy stood up from the lounger with a slight huff of effort. She smiled and waved at her two-and-a-half-year-old son Ajax, who admittedly looked as if he was splashing more than swimming, being tugged along in armbands by his father.

She plonked a sunhat on her head and went over to the edge of the pool, which was just one of the luxurious features of the Achilles Villa in the Krisakis Resort, which had opened a couple of years ago. This was the villa Sophy had suggested building at the top of the resort and it was the most sought-after for its views and privacy.

As Sophy had predicted, they were inundated with visitors looking to escape the far busier islands around them, and Krisakis was thriving and growing all the time.

Sometimes they themselves needed to escape, and they went out on the yacht that Apollo had bought at the auction those few years ago. He'd named it *Little Flame*, much to Sophy's delight.

She went down on her haunches. 'You are doing so well, my love. Papa is a good teacher, isn't he? He taught me how to swim too.'

Ajax, dark-haired and a handful, as only a child of Apollo could be, broke into giggles. 'Papa teaching Mama to swim—that's silly! You're a grown-up!'

Sophy saw Apollo's smirk and splashed some water at him. He said warningly, 'You'll pay for that, Kyria Vasilis.'

She was Kyria Vasilis again. Except officially this time. They'd got married here on Krisakis in the small Greek Orthodox church. The inevitable media interest in Apollo marrying his widow's twin sister had been handled well by his PR team and it had quickly faded from the news pages.

Sophy stood up now and undid the wraparound kaftan, dropping it to the ground. She saw the way Apollo's eyes narrowed on her and the inevitable flame in their depths.

Her own body—so attuned to his—tingled and fizzed with anticipation. Lord knew, she shouldn't be feeling sexy. She was eight months pregnant and the size of a small hippo but nothing was capable of diminishing their desire. Even Ajax's arrival had been precipitated by Apollo's very sensual brand of trying to 'hurry him along' when she'd been overdue with him.

She went over to the steps that led down into the pool and sat down, relishing the feel of the water cooling her sun-warmed skin. Apollo left Ajax splashing happily in the shallow end and came over to where she was, sliding his arms around her and stealing a kiss. Something they never got away with for long in front of their son.

He pulled back and sat beside her, putting a hand over her belly. The baby kicked. It was a girl. But they were keeping it a secret from Ajax. She put her hand over her husband's and they looked at each other, a wealth of emotion flowing between them.

They'd already been tested by grief when Sophy had lost their second baby at about four months to a miscarriage, almost a year ago now. But that experience had only made their bond even stronger.

Ajax's voice suddenly piped up with an imperious, 'Mama, come here! I want to show you something.'

Sophy smiled wryly at Apollo and moved into the water, swimming lazily over to her son, the way her husband had taught her.

Apollo looked at his wife and son playing and his heart was so full he didn't know how it didn't burst. But it didn't. It just grew and expanded every day. And in another month or so it would expand a lot more.

And what he'd found, thanks to his love for his wife and his family, was that it was always infinitely better to make love the goal. And not self-protection. Because the thought of not experiencing this beauty and love and joy… Well, that was more terrifying than anything.

* * * * *

Swept away by The Greek's Unknown Bride?
Lose yourself in these other stories by Abby Green!

An Innocent, A Seduction, A Secret
Awakened by the Scarred Italian
Confessions of a Pregnant Cinderella
Redeemed by His Stolen Bride

Available now!

WE HOPE YOU ENJOYED
THIS BOOK FROM

⬡ HARLEQUIN

PRESENTS

Escape to exotic locations where passion knows no bounds.

Welcome to the glamorous lives of royals and billionaires, where passion knows no bounds. Be swept into a world of luxury, wealth and exotic locations.

8 NEW BOOKS AVAILABLE EVERY MONTH!

COMING NEXT MONTH FROM

PRESENTS

Available May 19, 2020

#3817 CINDERELLA'S ROYAL SECRET
Once Upon a Temptation
by Lynne Graham
For innocent cleaner Izzy, accidentally interrupting her most exclusive client, Sheikh Rafiq, coming out of the shower is mortifying...yet their instantaneous attraction leads to the most amazing night of her life! But then she does a pregnancy test...

#3818 BEAUTY AND HER ONE-NIGHT BABY
Once Upon a Temptation
by Dani Collins
The first time Scarlett sees Javiero after their impassioned night together, she's in labor with his baby! She won't accept empty vows, even if she can't forget the pleasure they shared...and could share again!

#3819 SHY QUEEN IN THE ROYAL SPOTLIGHT
Once Upon a Temptation
by Natalie Anderson
To retain the throne he's sacrificed everything for, Alek *must* choose a bride. Hester's inner fire catches his attention. Alek sees the queen that she could truly become—but the real question is, can *she*?

#3820 CLAIMED IN THE ITALIAN'S CASTLE
Once Upon a Temptation
by Caitlin Crews
When innocent piano-playing Angelina must marry enigmatic Benedetto Franceschi, she *should* be terrified—his reputation precedes him. But their electrifying chemistry forges an unspoken connection. Dare she hope he could become the husband she deserves?

#3821 EXPECTING HIS BILLION-DOLLAR SCANDAL
Once Upon a Temptation
by Cathy Williams

Luca relished the fact his fling with Cordelia was driven by desire, not his wealth. Now their baby compels him to bring her into his sumptuous world. But to give Cordelia his heart? It's a price he can't pay...

#3822 TAMING THE BIG BAD BILLIONAIRE
Once Upon a Temptation
by Pippa Roscoe

Ella may be naive, but she's no pushover. Discovering Roman's lies, she can't pretend their passion-filled marriage never happened. He might see himself as a big bad wolf, but she knows he could be so much more...

#3823 THE FLAW IN HIS MARRIAGE PLAN
Once Upon a Temptation
by Tara Pammi

Family is *everything* to tycoon Vincenzo. The man who ruined his mother's life will pay. Vincenzo will wed his enemy's adopted daughter: Alessandra. The flaw in his plan? Their fiery attraction... and his need to protect her.

#3824 HIS INNOCENT'S PASSIONATE AWAKENING
Once Upon a Temptation
by Melanie Milburne

If there's a chance that marrying Artie will give his grandfather the will to live, Luca *must* do it. But he's determined to resist temptation. Until their scorching wedding kiss stirs the beauty to sensual new life! _____

HPCNMRB0520

SPECIAL EXCERPT FROM

HARLEQUIN

PRESENTS

The first time Scarlett sees Javiero after their impassioned night together she's in labour with his baby! But she won't accept empty vows—even if she can't forget the pleasure they shared...and could share again!

Read on for a sneak preview of Dani Collins's next story for Harlequin Presents,
Beauty and Her One-Night Baby.

Scarlett dropped her phone with a clatter.

She had been trying to call Kiara. Now she was taking in the livid claw marks across Javiero's face, each pocked on either side with the pinpricks of recently removed stitches. His dark brown hair was longer than she'd ever seen it, perhaps gelled back from the widow's peak at some point this morning, but it was mussed and held a jagged part. He wore a black eye patch like a pirate, its narrow band cutting a thin stripe across his temple and into his hair.

Maybe that's why his features looked as though they had been set askew? His mouth was...not right. His upper lip was uneven and the claw marks drew lines through his unkempt stubble all the way down into his neck.

That was dangerously close to his jugular! Dear God, he had nearly been killed.

She grasped at the edge of the sink, trying to stay on her feet while she grew so light-headed at the thought of him dying that she feared she would faint.

The ravages of his attack weren't what made him look so forbidding and grim, though, she computed through her haze of panic and anguish. No. The contemptuous glare in his one eye was for her. For this.

He flicked another outraged glance at her middle.

"I thought we were meeting in the boardroom." His voice sounded gravelly. Damaged as well? Or was that simply his true feelings toward her now? Deadly and completely devoid of any of the sensual admiration she'd sometimes heard in his tone.

Not that he'd ever been particularly warm toward her. He'd been aloof, indifferent, irritated, impatient, explosively passionate. Generous in the giving of pleasure. Of compliments. Then cold as she left. Disapproving. Malevolent.

Damningly silent.

And now he was…what? Ignoring that she was as big as a barn?

Her arteries were on fire with straight adrenaline, her heart pounding and her brain spinning with the way she was having to switch gears so fast. Her eyes were hot and her throat tight. Everything in her wanted to scream *help me*, but she'd been in enough tight spots to know this was all on her. Everything was always on her. She fought to keep her head and get through the next few minutes before she moved on to the next challenge.

Which was just a tiny trial called childbirth, but she would worry about that when she got to the hospital.

As the tingle of a fresh contraction began to pang in her lower back, she tightened her grip on the edge of the sink and gritted her teeth, trying to ignore the coming pain and hang on to what dregs of dignity she had left.

"I'm in labor," she said tightly. "It's yours."

Don't miss
Beauty and Her One-Night Baby.

Available June 2020 wherever
Harlequin Presents books and ebooks are sold.

Harlequin.com